'TIL DEATH DO US PART

THE VOWS BOOK 3

HEIDI RENEE MASON

BOOKS

Always Hope (stand alone)

Love At First Crepe (Sweet Escape 1)

Just Double the Recipe (Sweet Escape 2)

To Have and To Hold (The Vows 1)

For Better or For Worse (The Vows 2)

'Til Death Do Us Part (The Vows 3)

DEDICATION

This book is dedicated to my three daughters and women everywhere. You are stronger than you know. Be your own hero.

PART ONE
NOVEMBER

Ohio
"Your feet will bring you to where your heart is." –Irish Proverb

ONE

Pacing back and forth in his tiny prison cell, Xavier Smith resembled a caged tiger. Sleek, powerful, and deadly, he was a man of action. It was how he operated, and nothing, including two years in prison, could change that. He smoothed the wrinkles from his orange jumpsuit and rested his large muscular physique on the steel bedstead. The paper-thin mat the prison had the nerve to call a mattress did little to cushion the bulk of his ever-increasing body.

The only good thing he'd discovered about being locked up was that he had more time to work out. He had nearly doubled his size since he'd been at the Ohio State Penitentiary. As soon as he figured a way out of the joint, he planned to put all that muscle mass to good use. Other than the workout equipment, there were no amenities at all in prison. For a man used to every creature comfort money could buy, that was simply unacceptable.

What made Xavier's situation even worse was being trapped in a cell, day after miserable day, when he'd done nothing wrong. The whole situation had been a mistake. During the seemingly endless passage of time in the state pen, he'd had plenty of time to think about all of it, and he'd come to one conclusion—he'd had enough.

Xavier vaulted from the bed and paced in frustration. The only thing he was guilty of was trying to make his dream of possessing Emma a reality. He was simply a man in love. He couldn't understand why that was an issue.

He slammed his fist into the brick wall. Pain flared across his knuckles, but the blood smeared on the wall eased some of the pent-up anger that boiled in his gut. When he'd broken into her house, he'd only been trying to show her how much he cared, and he would have convinced her if Liam O'Reilly hadn't interfered.

That man was forever getting in the way. He'd brain-washed Emma into believing Xavier was a monster, but that would all be set right in no time at all. He was sure of it. All he needed was some time alone with Emma to convince her of the truth. Then they could finally begin their lives together.

Xavier wiped his bloody fist on his jumpsuit and took some deep breaths. He couldn't allow his demons to control him.

He slumped onto the bed once again and began counting the bricks. He'd counted them so many times that he had each one memorized. All he could do hour after hour was pace and count bricks. No wonder he was losing control. It's why the voices had started whispering into his ear again. He was having a harder time quieting them than ever before. His mind began to spin again as he reclined on the thin mattress and laced his hands behind his head. His knuckles were bleeding, but he didn't care.

He had to think of a way out. Last year he'd hatched a nearly foolproof plan, but that hadn't worked out as he'd anticipated. Morgan Turner, the gorgeous, conniving woman who'd fancied herself in love with him, was supposed to be pulling the strings from the outside. If she would have just stuck to the rules and carried out his simple instructions, everything would have been fine. Instead, the stupid woman went off the deep end and tried to kill Emma. Luckily his beloved Emma had escaped and killed Morgan instead. Good riddance to bad rubbish.

One thing Xavier had learned during his unfortunate incarceration was that if he wanted something done right, he had to do it himself. He couldn't trust anyone.

He'd made a lucrative career stealing jewels, priceless artwork, and ancient artifacts, and he had connections all around the world. He'd given it a lot of thought, and he'd come to the conclusion that all of his contacts were too inept to deal with someone as precious as Emma. Experience had taught him that the only person he could count on was himself. Being locked up in a cell was going to make his plan a bit more difficult, but Xavier had always been a determined man. His will and fortitude were the exact traits that made him an excellent thief. His intelligence would get him out of his current circumstances and into the life he wanted—one that included Emma.

It might take some time, but he was going to make it happen. Emma belonged to him, and there wasn't a thing Liam or anyone else could do about it. The past was in the past, and Xavier Smith would not fail.

A slow, devious grin pulled at the corners of his mouth until it covered his entire face. He chuckled to himself and pictured how perfect it would be. His chortle transformed into a cackle until his maniacal laughter reverberated off the concrete walls. Before long, every prisoner on the entire cell block had joined in.

TWO

"So it sounds like the nightmares are becoming less frequent. Is that right, Emma?" Dr. Oslo, Emma's therapist, inquired.

"Yes, I guess that's true. When I first came to see you, I was having vivid dreams every night. Now I only have them once a week or so. I guess that means I'm cured, right?" Emma smiled.

"Let's not rush things. You know, most people never come close to experiencing the trauma you've endured."

"True, but a lot of people have bad things happen to them."

"Maybe you don't understand the scope of what has happened to you, Emma. Your husband, Jacob, was a jewel thief who was having an affair with your neighbor Veronica. He'd been running from the authorities for years before Liam caught on to him. Jacob died in a plane crash, leaving you alone and pregnant with no money to take care of your children. Then your parents died. Veronica's husband, Xavier, the man who is obsessed with you, sits in prison for trying to abduct you. Then his mentally disturbed girlfriend,

Morgan, tried to kill you. A year in therapy isn't going to make it all go away. It's not like waving a magic wand."

Dr. Oslo, a kind woman in her mid-sixties, peered at Emma over the rims of her square glasses. The list of horrible events was painful to revisit, but Dr. Oslo had always been very honest.

"I know. I get it. Really, I do. But I told you from the beginning that therapy isn't my thing."

Emma was determined to avoid the business of dredging up her past. She shook her head and tried not to meet the doctor's eyes, which was difficult since they were seated in overstuffed armchairs facing one another. It actually surprised Emma that, even after coming twice a week for an entire year, she'd had the courage to follow through with therapy. Confronting her feelings made her uncomfortable; she preferred to ignore them and hope they would go away.

Dr. Oslo scribbled some notes on a yellow legal pad as Emma looked around the familiar office. The cheerful pale blue walls and lacy curtains seemed better suited to a cozy farmhouse than a psychiatrist's office, but Emma liked it. The serene watercolor paintings and framed photos of Dr. Oslo's cats on the large mahogany desk made Emma feel as if she was in the doctor's home, not a sterile room being analyzed.

"You're doing well, Emma. None of this has been easy for you. However—" Dr. Oslo waited until Emma met her eyes. "—I recommend that you continue coming to see me once a week on your own, and once a week with Liam. I believe our sessions are doing you both a great deal of good. Can you agree to that?"

Dr. Oslo had a way of making Emma want to do exactly as she suggested. The woman was very good at her job.

"Yes. If you think it's for the best, I'll keep coming. Even though I complain about it, our talks are helping. I'm much calmer, I'm better able to see when my anxiety level is rising, and I can't argue with the fact that my nightmares are decreasing. You win." Emma nodded slowly and conceded to Dr. Oslo's plans.

"It's not about winning or losing, or being wrong or right. It's about you getting healthy and dealing with the fact that you have a lot of heavy issues to confront. Most people aren't equipped to handle that alone, Emma. You haven't failed at anything. Quite the contrary—admitting you need help means you've succeeded."

The wise therapist scribbled some notes into Emma's file, closed it, and neatly folded her hands on her lap.

"All right. Liam and I will see you at our appointment in two days, then." Emma gathered her purse, fished for her keys, and rose to her feet.

Dr. Oslo stood as well and led Emma to the door of her office. "Do you and Liam have big plans for Thanksgiving?"

"We do. As a matter of fact, I'm going to have a full house. Liam's parents, sister, brother-in-law, and nieces are all coming in from Chicago. His cousin, Colin, and his aunt and uncle from Ireland will be there, and Sadie's parents are flying in from New York. Of course, Sadie will be there, too." Emma grinned widely.

"Oh my, that sounds lovely."

"Yes, the girls and I will be busy cooking for the next week, but it's so nice to have family to celebrate with again. Since my parents died, the holidays have always felt a bit hollow to me. Everything feels different this year," Emma explained.

"You have much to be thankful for. I'll see you in a couple of days."

Dr. Oslo waved goodbye as Emma exited the building and jumped into her SUV. She started the vehicle and backed out of the parking lot. Dr. Oslo was right about one thing—

Emma had insisted all along that she didn't need therapy, but it was working wonders for her state of mind.

After Daisy was born, Emma entered a frightening mental state. Some people suggested it was postpartum depression, but Emma knew it went even deeper. She was afraid of her own shadow. She couldn't sleep at all, and she barely ate. She was perpetually cranky and exhausted, and most days she ended up in tears over the simplest of things. Some days she couldn't even bring herself to get out of bed.

She couldn't take care of her children, her husband, or herself. It all boiled down to Emma not knowing how to deal with the fact that she'd killed someone. It didn't seem to matter that Morgan drugged, abducted, and chained Emma to a mattress, then starved and nearly killed her and her unborn baby in the process. She still felt guilty. Emma clearly understood that if she hadn't killed Morgan, the woman would have surely killed her, but the fact that she'd taken another life still haunted her every day. Emma couldn't quite wrap her brain around how she was supposed to go on with business as usual after that.

Liam, Colin, and Sadie had been terrified for Emma, and they'd begged her to listen to reason. After fighting them for the entire first year of Daisy's life, they finally convinced her to get some help. She'd been reluctant to seek therapy, but everyone had been right. She needed help, and that's exactly what she'd received from Dr. Oslo.

Finally, two years after the horrific ordeal with Morgan, Emma's life was looking up again. She was more and more the old Emma every day. There was still a long way to go, as Dr. Oslo always reminded her, but with the support of her family, she'd get there.

Glancing at the clock in her vehicle, Emma noted that she'd be home just in time to get the girls off the bus and relieve Sadie, who was babysitting Daisy.

Normally Liam watched the baby during Emma's appointments, but he was out of town working on a case. He'd been gone for a week, and he would be back in less than twenty-four hours, not that Emma was counting. She was anxious to have her husband home again. Working away from Beckland was part of his job, but having him home set everything right in her world.

With Liam gone, Sadie had graciously offered to watch Daisy so Emma wouldn't have to cancel her therapy appointment. Colin was in Chicago for two days, and having something to occupy Sadie's time kept her from pining after him too much. Colin and Sadie were inseparable, practically joined at the hip. They were adorable.

Colin had extended his visit to the United States, and Emma knew Sadie was the reason. Seeing her best friend in love made Emma's heart happy. Sadie was studying the history and customs of Ireland, and she was taking an Irish-Gaelic language course online so she could better understand Colin's homeland.

After years of faithfully taking care of Emma and her daughters, Sadie was finally on the path to getting her own happily ever after.

Emma pulled into her driveway and turned off the car. Through the large bay windows, she saw Sadie and Daisy playing on the floor of the living room. Emma, who had been blessed with four healthy children, wondered if someday soon Sadie would have children of her own. She'd been a co-parent of Emma's children since Lily was born, and Emma knew she'd make a fabulous mother.

Emma smiled as Sadie held Daisy's hands while they bounced around the room. The school bus rounded the corner, and Emma felt the familiar excitement as Lily, Rose, and Dahlia crossed the street and ran through the front yard.

Having her family together was Emma's favorite part of the day.

As they headed inside, Emma counted her blessings. Her life had nearly been stolen from her twice, and she was determined to hold it closely. She'd finally found her way out of the darkness, and she was never going back again.

THREE

"Honey, I'm home," Emma called playfully to Sadie as she and the girls walked through the front door.

The warm air inside was a stark contrast to the brisk November winds outside. Snow was coming; Emma could feel it in her bones. She ushered the girls inside and closed the door quickly.

"The baby and I are in the living room, dear," Sadie answered with a laugh in her voice.

"Girls, do not drop your coats and backpacks in the middle of the hallway. Put them where they belong, and get started on your homework," Emma instructed her daughters.

"C'mon, Mom, can't we do it later?" Lily whined.

Emma's oldest was a full-blown teenager. She was thirteen going on thirty, and her favorite extracurricular activity was pushing her mother's buttons.

"You know the rules, Lily. Homework gets done before anything else. I don't know why we have to discuss it every day." Emma sent Lily a warning look. Once she started arguing, her two younger sisters would follow suit.

"Fine. Come on, Rose and Dahlia, let's go do what Mom

said." Lily rolled her eyes dramatically, but did as her mother asked.

"I'll check in on Sadie and Daisy, and then I'll fix you all a snack. You can do your homework in the kitchen."

Emma walked down the hall toward the living room. The minute Daisy saw her mother, she toddled across the well-worn hardwood floor with her chubby arms outstretched. The baby had been walking since she was nine months old. Knowing she would probably be her last child, Emma hadn't been in a hurry for Daisy to reach any of the usual milestones. Always trying to keep up with her older sisters, though, the littlest O'Reilly girl had been the fastest at everything. Emma loved each and every baby stage, and it made her sad that it was going by so quickly. Before long, she would be just as grown up as her sisters.

"Hi, Daisy. Mama missed you." Emma bent down and lightly kissed her daughter's red curls. Daisy's blue eyes, exactly like Liam's, sparkled with delight. She giggled in response and threw her little arms around Emma's neck.

"Mama, you home," Daisy chirped in her sweet two-year-old's voice.

"I think she missed you." Sadie grinned as she picked up the blocks they'd been stacking.

"How did it go? Was she a handful?" Emma flopped onto the cozy leather sofa and placed Daisy on her lap.

"She was an angel, as always. Busy, but good." Sadie collapsed next to Emma. "How was your session?"

"Productive. I'm feeling stronger every day, although Dr. Oslo assures me that I'm not cured yet." Emma rolled her eyes dramatically, as Lily often did.

"Maybe not, but you're in a much better place than you were last year."

"That's true. I'm glad you and Liam insisted I see her. I can't imagine where I'd be right now if I hadn't."

"We love you." Sadie smiled.

"Love you, too." Emma returned the smile and sighed. "I need to fix the girls a snack. They're probably starving by now."

She placed Daisy on her hip and headed into the kitchen. Sadie followed. The kitchen was Emma's favorite room in the large Victorian house that once belonged to her parents. Since she'd owned it, she'd done a bit of remodeling, but she refused to change the kitchen. It was exactly the way her mother had left it. Spacious and well lit, the warm, wooden cabinets and large, well-loved farmhouse table situated in front of the sunny bay window gave the room a homey feel.

Grabbing Daisy's high chair, she sat the toddler inside and placed some crackers on the tray to keep the little girl occupied while Emma sliced apples. After arranging the sliced fruit on four plates, she added a dollop of peanut butter on each one. She then delivered three of the plates to her daughters, who were hard at work at the kitchen table, and sat the fourth one on the kitchen counter. Sadie took a seat on the swiveling bar stool beside Emma, and they munched while they chatted.

"I can't wait for Liam to get home tomorrow. He's been gone a week. I'd forgotten how hard this single parent thing was. I don't know how I did it all those years," she grumbled.

"You're Superwoman, of course. You also had me." Sadie grinned as she chomped on an apple slice.

"That is the truth of it. I couldn't have done it without you," Emma agreed.

"I miss Colin. He's running some mysterious errand in Chicago. He's only been gone a couple of days, but it feels like years. Is that pathetic or what?" Sadie whined.

"It's not pathetic. I know exactly what you mean. I feel lost when Liam isn't around. I wonder what Colin is up to in Chicago?"

"I have no idea. He was awfully vague about why he went. He's staying with Liam's parents, so maybe he just wanted to visit his aunt and uncle. But that seems strange because they're coming here next week. I'm trying not to be a clingy girlfriend, but I'm failing miserably."

"I still can't believe you guys have been together for two years. I never imagined you'd hit it off so well when Colin came from Ireland to help Liam. He was only supposed to stay for six months, but he's still here, two years later." Emma grinned and swiped her apple slice through the peanut butter.

"Maybe I had something to do with it," Sadie replied, but she sounded unsure.

"What do you mean, maybe? Colin is crazy about you! Of course you're the reason he stayed in America." Emma couldn't believe her best friend would doubt that fact.

"I know he cares for me. But Emma, I...."

Emma knew immediately that something was bothering her best friend. She was determined to get to the bottom of whatever it was.

"Lily, can you please keep an eye on Daisy while you do your homework? I need to talk to Sadie for just a minute."

Lily rolled her eyes at her mother's request but nodded her blonde head in agreement.

Emma grabbed Sadie's hand and led her back into the living room where they both sat on the couch. The gray sky, which was visible from the large bay window, seemed to match her friend's mood.

"What's going on, Sadie? Spill it," Emma demanded.

"I don't know what's wrong with me. It's just that I... I'm scared. I love Colin so much, Emma. I don't know what I'm going to do without him. I never thought I could feel this way about someone, but I'm a blubbering mess just thinking about what I'm going to do once he leaves." Sadie's beautiful blue eyes filled with tears.

Emma took Sadie's trembling hand. "Honey, I know Colin has to go back to Ireland after Thanksgiving, and the thought of it is tearing you up inside. But I'm sure he's just as upset about it as you are. You guys are going to work this out."

"How are we going to work it out, Emma? It feels impossible! I can't leave my job. I'm contracted with the library for another two years. And I love Beckland. It's my home. I could never leave you and the girls. Besides, even if I were willing to go, Colin hasn't asked me to. We've never talked about what happens once he goes home to Ireland." Sadie's tears fell, one by one, as she spoke.

"You can't doubt that he loves you, Sadie." Emma bit her lip in frustration.

"He says he loves me, and I believe him. But what if that means something different to him than it does to me? What if mine is the forever kind of love and his isn't?" She shrugged her slender shoulders and picked at invisible lint on her yoga pants.

Emma squeezed her friend's hand. "Have you talked to Colin about your concerns?"

Sadie responded by shaking her head wildly. "No! I don't want to be a clingy girlfriend who needs constant reassurance. I swore I would never be that girl, but right now that's just what I want to do. I want him to promise me that we'll always be together. That's unrealistic, isn't it? I knew when I met him that he was here temporarily. Ohio isn't his home, but it's mine." Sadie wiped the tears from her eyes.

"Oh, sweetie, I wish I had a perfect answer for you, but I don't. All I can say is that I would bet my life on the fact that Colin feels exactly the same way you feel about him. I don't know how, but I know it's going to work out for you two. I can feel it." Emma hugged Sadie closely and felt the worry and sadness swirling around inside her friend.

"I'm not sure about anything anymore." Sadie sighed heavily.

Emma and Sadie had always described themselves as being one soul in two bodies. They were so close that they could feel one another's emotions. Emma's heart constricted with empathy for her friend. She remembered when her relationship with Liam was new and uncertain. She understood all too well what it felt like to be so much in love that it hurt. More than anything, Emma wanted to make everything better for Sadie, but she couldn't. Sadie and Colin needed to navigate their relationship themselves. All Emma could do was support them, no matter what happened.

"Is this how it was when you fell in love with Liam?" Sadie took a deep breath, smoothed her hair, and tried to compose herself.

"If you mean that one minute it felt like my life was some kind of fairy tale, and the next it felt like I was being swallowed whole by my own emotions, then yes, that's it. That's what falling in love feels like." Emma wondered when she'd become an expert on love.

"It's so hard. Tell me it will all be worth it." Sadie looked at her friend for assurance.

"When love is right, you must fight to hold on to it. Don't let anyone take it away from you. That feeling doesn't come along every day. And Sadie, I'm sure Colin is the right one for you."

"That's the thing, Em, I'm sure he's the right one for me, too. But maybe I'm not the right one for him." Sadie shrugged again.

"I don't think you have anything to worry about. My mom always said not to borrow trouble, and that's exactly what you're doing. You're imagining possibilities that don't even exist. Colin has another two weeks in the United States. Don't waste them by worrying about what may or may not happen. Enjoy every second you have with him." Emma encouraged Sadie with another quick squeeze.

"You're right, Em. Thanks for talking some sense into me. I feel like I'm turning into one of those sappy women who can't remember how to live on her own once she finds a man. Ugh!" Sadie gasped. "I *am* turning into one of those women, aren't I?"

"Honey, you're just fine. Falling in love messes with the best of us." Emma smiled.

"It's beautiful and awful at the same time. How does anyone survive it?"

"I'm not sure we do. The jury is still out. C'mon, let's check on the girls. It's awfully quiet in there, and that's never a good thing."

The women headed back into the kitchen. Colin would be back in town soon, and Emma decided that maybe she and Liam needed to have a little talk with him. Emma knew Colin loved Sadie, but if he hurt her best friend, he was going to have a problem on his hands.

FOUR

THE NEXT AFTERNOON, EMMA WAS LOADING THE DISHWASHER and singing a song to Daisy when Liam's Mustang pulled into the driveway. He'd bought a new car after the last one was totaled, and he'd opted for red. The color suited him perfectly. The engine roared, and her heart pounded in anticipation of seeing her husband after what had proven to be a very long week. Emma grabbed Daisy from the floor where she was playing and placed the toddler on her hip as she cooed, "Daddy's home."

Daisy smiled and Emma glanced at the clock, taking note that the other girls would be home from school soon. They would also be excited to see their father. The O'Reilly clan enjoyed their family time, and it just wasn't the same when one of them was missing.

Emma walked down the hallway carrying Daisy. She opened the front door as Liam sprinted up the porch steps toward them. The smile on his face was a mile wide. Emma felt like a giddy schoolgirl, but she didn't care. She'd missed her husband, and she was ecstatic that he was finally home.

Liam wrapped Daisy and Emma in a fierce hug before

smothering his wife's eager mouth with a thousand kisses. She never grew tired of feeling his lips on hers. Kissing Liam was like sipping a sweet elixir that made her feel like a teenager again, not the thirtysomething mother of four she was.

"Dada," Daisy squealed as Liam lifted her in his arms. She tangled her tiny fists in her father's dark hair, pulling his face toward hers. She obviously wanted his attention, and she wasn't afraid to make her opinion known.

"Hey, baby girl." Liam smiled as he planted a soft kiss on the top of his daughter's head. "Were you good for Mama while I was gone?"

Daisy answered by granting him a huge smile and showing her dimple that was an exact replica of his. Liam was a wonderful father to all their girls, and that endearing quality just further cemented Emma's love for him.

"Daisy was a very good girl while you were away, but I'm happy you're home. Doing all of this without you is not easy." Between keeping up with her coffee shop, Morning Glory, and chasing after four daughters who moved at the speed of light, Emma was beat. "You'll be happy to know that I did find the energy to make your favorite dinner, though." She smiled at her husband.

"You made lasagna?" Liam's blue eyes sparkled in anticipation, and Emma couldn't help but laugh at his obvious excitement.

"I did. It was a labor of love. Daisy wasn't happy about me dividing my attention between her and the pasta, but somehow I managed," she answered.

"I don't suppose you made that delicious cheesy garlic bread to go along with it, did you?" Liam asked with a hopeful look in his eyes.

"As a matter of fact, I did." Emma giggled as her husband's eyes widened with obvious delight.

Liam placed Daisy on the large Persian rug on the living room floor before wrapping his wife in his arms. "You are far too good to me. I don't know how I got so lucky."

"The feeling is mutual, Mr. O'Reilly. You're pretty amazing yourself." Emma fisted her hands in his dark curly hair and pulled his face to hers. When their lips met, Emma closed her eyes and relished the feeling of having Liam next to her again. Butterflies danced inside, and she wondered if the giddiness he made her feel would ever go away. She hoped not.

When the kiss ended, he smoothed her hair from her face and winked at her, a silent promise that they would pick up where they left off later. Just then, the school bus arrived. Emma glanced out the window and saw the girls running through the front yard. Liam walked to the door amidst squeals of delight and proclamations of "Daddy's home!"

The girls bombarded their father with hugs and kisses, and all three attempted to talk to him at once. He smiled and welcomed them into his arms, clearly happy to see them. He helped them get settled at the kitchen table to begin homework before grabbing Daisy and placing her on his lap. He remained close by, answering Lily's questions about the Civil War, helping Dahlia solve a difficult math equation, and assuring Rose that finishing her homework on time was definitely a good idea. He fed Daisy Cheerios, keeping her quiet and content while her sisters worked.

He jumped seamlessly back into his parenting duties as if he'd never been gone. Emma recognized it as his attempt to give her a much-needed break.

"Em, why don't you go upstairs and soak in a hot bath for a while? You already made dinner, and I have things under control in the homework department. Take some time for yourself. I know you have to be tired," Liam suggested.

"I am tired, but it's only three thirty in the afternoon. It's a little early for a bath, isn't it?"

"It's never too early to enjoy some relaxation after being a single mom for a week. Go."

"All right, if you're sure," she hedged.

"Go, Emma. Take the break when it's offered."

"Okay, but first I wanted to ask you something about Colin and Sadie." Emma had been worried about Sadie since their chat yesterday, and she couldn't rest until she talked to Liam about it.

"Can it wait? You should seize your moment of peace and quiet while you have the chance. You know the natives will be restless soon," he said with a smile.

"No, it can't wait. I'm worried about Sadie. She's upset that Colin will be going back to Ireland soon, and I assured her that he was worried about it, too. Do you think I'm right? You know him better than I do. Is Colin in love with Sadie?"

Emma wouldn't normally have a discussion about adult relationships in front of the girls, but she needed answers. Besides, they knew all about what was going on, and they were probably wondering what would happen to Aunt Sadie once Uncle Colin went home to Galway.

"Emma, you've seen them together. Isn't it obvious?" Liam grinned at his wife's blatant attempt to meddle.

"Come on, Liam. Humor me. Do you think we should have a talk with Colin? If he breaks my best friend's heart, he's going to have to deal with me. I don't care if he is your cousin." Emma narrowed her eyes at her husband in warning.

"Honey, they're both adults. It's not our place to interfere. Can you just let things play out between them as they're supposed to?" Liam sighed, and Emma could tell that the subject of his cousin's love life wasn't his favorite topic for discussion.

"Fine then, if you won't talk to Colin, I'll do it myself." Emma placed her hands on her hips in determination.

"No, Emma. Promise me you won't interfere."

"Why?" Emma narrowed her eyes again at Liam's reaction. "Do you know something I don't?"

"Just promise me," Liam repeated.

"Fine, I won't interfere. *For now.*" Emma's rigid shoulders relaxed as she sighed heavily and nodded in agreement.

"Thank you. Now you should go get that bubble bath while you're still able to escape." Liam smiled again.

Emma rolled her eyes as she headed upstairs for a bit of respite. It went against her better judgment to just leave things alone, but she'd promised her husband she would stay out of it. She hoped their relationship worked out, because she wouldn't stand for anyone, not even Colin, breaking Sadie's heart.

FIVE

XAVIER SMITH WALKED BESIDE ROBINSON DURANT, HIS FELLOW inmate, in the prison courtyard. He slowed his usual brisk pace a bit in order to match the older man's strides step for step. He hated slowing down when he had the opportunity to exercise to his full potential, but the conversation at hand was an important one, and because of that, he would make an exception.

"Why would I want to go and do something as dumb as that, Smith?" the older man, Durant, asked through his crooked yellow teeth.

Durant's grizzled facial features spoke of the many years the man had spent behind bars. Frizzy, disheveled gray hair adorned his head, and weather-worn leathery skin encased with wrinkles was the canvas for his eyes, which were twin pools of inky black anger. Even though Durant was at least thirty years Xavier's senior, he was surprisingly physically fit, thanks to the prison weight room, where he and Xavier had first become acquainted.

In spite of his age, Durant wasn't a man anyone would want to meet in a dark alley. Over the past couple of years in prison, Xavier had come to respect the older man, and he knew Durant was the perfect partner to set his newly hatched plan into motion.

"If you agree to help me, I intend to make it well worth your while, Durant." Xavier smiled slyly as he answered the question he'd been anticipating.

"How do you plan to do that? I've spent twenty years behind bars for armed robbery, and I'm set to get out next week. What could you possibly offer that would make me want to give that up?" Durant laughed. It was a bone-chilling sound that drifted away in the cold November wind.

"I'm offering you wealth beyond your wildest imagination—more money than you could ever hope to make on your own. As you said, you've been a prisoner for twenty years. How do you plan to support yourself once you're out of here?" Xavier had been rehearsing his speech for days, ever since he'd figured out exactly how he was going to get out of this joint.

"The way I supported myself before I came." Durant snorted. "I'll just take what I need to get by."

"I'm sure you are very good at what you do, my friend, but why work so hard when you don't have to? I'm offering you a lifestyle you could otherwise only dream of." Xavier was laying the bait.

"You say you can give me more money than I could imagine. How are you going to do that? In case you've forgotten, Smith, you're behind bars too," Durant retorted as he shook his head in irritation.

"Here's the deal, Durant. I've lived an interesting and highly complex life. Before I got caught, I established quite an underground network of associates. I was the absolute best at what I did. With that expertise came an impressive amount of wealth. It's sitting there, in offshore bank accounts, just waiting for me to get out of here. I have more money than you could dream of, and I'm happy to give you a large chunk of it—if you agree." Xavier was setting the hook, and he hoped to reel in a whopper.

"Why should I trust you? How do I know you're not lying to me?" Durant stopped walking and scratched his head, obviously considering Xavier's words.

"Well, that's the tricky part. You see, I don't have any proof to offer you, other than my word. From one con artist to another, you're just going to have to trust me."

That was the part Xavier had been dreading. He knew he was asking a lot of the other man, and if circumstances were reversed, he would probably laugh off the idea and call it pure craziness. But Xavier was counting on the fact that Durant was indeed a little crazy, and that he was probably feeling a bit uncertain and desperate given his current situation. He was hoping the man might jump at the chance for some financial stability, whatever the cost.

"Tell me again how this is going to work," Durant replied slowly.

"It's simple. Foolproof. You're set to be released next week. You've served your time, and you will soon be a free man. I have many more years left on my sentence, but I have some business that needs my immediate attention. I have to get out of here. If you'll help me, I'll make it worth your while," Xavier began.

"Go on."

"Here's how it's going to work. You fight me."

"What? You're crazy, man." Durant shook his head and started to walk away.

"No, wait, hear me out." The desperation in Xavier's voice caused Durant to turn around.

"I'm listening." Durant put his hand on his hip and sighed loudly, but he stayed put.

Xavier took a deep breath and continued, "You'll be a free

man soon, so they can't touch you. Tomorrow during yard time, I'll start in on you over the weights. We fight, and make it look real. I'll pull a shiv and you 'disarm' me during the fight. I need you to stab me here." Xavier gestured to a spot just below his left shoulder. "It's not life threatening, but the infirmary will have to do an MRI offsite at the local ER. I've made friends with a guard willing to trade a favor for a healthy donation. He'll make sure the infirmary follows through and escort me to the hospital. He'll take a few hits to make it look like he tried to stop me, but he'll ensure my escape. I have other friends on the outside to guarantee that my exit from the hospital is secure."

"Let me get this straight." Durant squinted one eye at Xavier, as if he could read his inner thoughts. "You want to pay me to stab you? Why not just pick the fight without telling me? You know I wouldn't back down."

"Because, my friend," Xavier said with a rueful smile, "I want to make certain that I live to see the ER. I want to control where you inflict damage, and I don't want you to kill me."

Durant nodded slowly, as if the lightbulb had finally gone off in his brain. He rubbed his stubbled face as he considered the plan. "What's my guarantee you won't hurt me? Or that I won't get thrown in solitary for the fight?"

Xavier laid his hand over his heart. "You have my word, friend. I need out, and I have no beef with you. And I'll make sure my guard friend keeps you in your cell until your release date."

"And then how do I get the money?" Durant's black eyes shone with excitement, and Xavier knew he was in.

"I'm going to leave you with a contact name and phone number. He'll meet you here the day you're released, get your money to you, and give you a ride wherever you need to go. I promise you, there will be a lot of money if you help me."

"What about you? Where will you be?"

"It's hard to tell where I'll be by that time. Where I end up is all going to depend on one very important woman." Xavier's gray eyes glistened as he thought of Emma.

Durant began pacing back and forth across the hard, frozen ground of the prison yard. Xavier could see he was considering his request. It was all finally within his reach.

"So, what do you think? Are you in?" the younger inmate questioned.

"I'll probably regret this, but yeah, I'm in. But I'll warn you, if you double-cross me, you're going to be sorry, Smith," Durant growled.

"I have no plans to double-cross you, my friend. What I want is worth far more than the money I intend to give you and the crooked guards. I will be happy to pay the price." Xavier smiled.

"I can't think of anything that would convince me to part with that much money. You must be crazy." Durant chuckled in glee, seeming confident he was getting the better end of the deal.

"I may very well be crazy, but Durant, some things in life you just can't put a price tag on, and I've found one. I will do anything within my power to get what I want," Xavier replied as he shook his partner's hand, sealing the deal.

He couldn't believe his luck. This time next week, the day after Thanksgiving, he would be well on his way to beginning his new life with Emma. It just didn't get any better than that.

SIX

Emma wiped the sweat from her forehead and continued rolling out the dough. She'd already made four pumpkin pies, and she was finally on the last one. It had been a marathon cooking day, but the end was finally in sight. The turkey was prepped to go into the oven the following morning, the noodles were drying on the counter, potatoes were peeled, diced, and ready to be boiled and mashed, and the desserts were nearly complete. Everything else could be finished early Thanksgiving morning.

Emma was grateful that she'd had extra hands to help her out, so she'd tried to prepare as much as possible in advance. She couldn't remember the last time she'd made such a feast. Normally it was just her little family for the holidays, but she was expecting a houseful. Even though the workload was mountainous, she couldn't have been happier.

Glancing across the kitchen at Sadie, who was loading the dishwasher for the third time, Emma sighed. Her friend had a faraway look on her lovely face, and Emma's heart went out to her. Colin's time in the United States was quickly drawing to an end, and Sadie was beside herself with worry about what would happen next. Emma had done her best to keep Sadie busy, hoping to keep her friend's mind occupied with food preparation and off Colin's departure, but it clearly wasn't working. Sadie had been standing at the sink rinsing the same dish for the past five minutes.

"Sadie, honey, I think the dish can go into the dishwasher now," Emma gently coaxed her friend from her daydream.

"Huh? Oh, yeah, I guess you're right." Sadie turned off the faucet and placed the dish in the rack. "Where are the girls? Weren't they just here?"

"They went upstairs to take their showers and get ready for bed about thirty minutes ago. What's on your mind?" Emma asked, although she already knew the answer.

"I was just thinking about… I don't know… everything, I guess." Sadie pushed the button to begin the wash cycle on the dishwasher, dried her hands on the kitchen towel, and flopped down onto the bar stool in front of Emma.

"I know. You're thinking about Colin leaving, right?"

"Yes. That's all I can think about. I know I should be focused on the time we have together. I mean, tomorrow is Thanksgiving. It's the time to be thankful, not mope around because of some guy." Sadie rolled her eyes.

"We all know Colin is way more than just some guy," Emma replied.

"He is. Oh, Emmy, I just love him so much. How am I going to live without him when he goes back?" Sadie buried her head in her hands.

"How do you know you're going to have to? Do you think he's just going to go back to Galway and you're never going to hear from him again? Is that what you're afraid of?" Emma couldn't believe how upset Sadie was.

"Yes, I'm afraid of everything. Sometimes I think it would have been better if I'd never met him. It would have been easier if I'd never known how amazing it could feel to be with a man like him. Now that I know, he's ruined me for regular life." Sadie sighed.

"I can't stand to see you so upset, Sadie." Emma patted her friend's hand.

"Oh, and you know what else? On top of the fact that he's leaving, I also have to meet his parents for the first time tomorrow. His parents! What if they hate me?" Sadie was starting to sound paranoid, so Emma tried to rein her in.

"His parents are not going to hate you, Sadie. What is there to dislike? You're a nearly perfect human being." Emma laughed at the ridiculousness of Sadie's statement.

"They probably wanted him to date some Irish girl, not an American librarian," Sadie spat.

"You are a beautiful, caring, intelligent, independent woman, and any man—or his parents, for that matter— would consider themselves lucky to know you."

"I don't know, Em. Colin is so close to his parents. If they don't like me, that's just the final nail in my coffin." She shook her head and chewed on her nails.

"Hey, I know just how you feel. I remember meeting Duncan and Eliza, Liam's parents, for the first time. I was terrified that they wouldn't like me. I was worried they would think Liam was crazy for marrying a widow with three kids. I couldn't have been more wrong. I was worried for no reason. The O'Reillys are fantastic people, who have welcomed me and the girls with open arms. It'll be just the same for you."

"I hope so, because if Dylan and Fionnula tell their son that I'm not good enough for him, I don't stand a chance."

"You'll see. Tomorrow is going to be a fabulous day. We're going to eat way too much food and spend the day hanging out with our families. Aren't you excited that your parents are flying in? We haven't seen them since last summer," Emma said, attempting to change the subject.

"Yeah, it'll be good to see them. I was surprised when they called out of the blue last week and said they were coming in for Thanksgiving. I'm not sure what brought on the impromptu visit, but I'll take it. They're usually traveling overseas this time of year, so I didn't expect to see them until July."

Sadie's parents never came to Ohio in the winter. They hated the cold weather.

"Well, they probably just missed you and wanted to get in an extra visit over the holidays," Emma assured her friend.

"I hope so. What if something's wrong with one of them?" Sadie continued chewing her nails and winced when she nipped a little too closely and got the skin.

"There you go again, borrowing trouble. When did you become such a Negative Nelly?" Emma couldn't believe how glum Sadie was.

"Ugh, I know. I can hear myself saying all of these crazy things, and I realize I'm being ridiculous, but I can't stop! I need to just glue my mouth shut or something. Better yet, I'll just stuff it full of a few more of these cookies you made." Sadie grabbed a peanut butter cookie off the counter and took a giant bite.

About that time, Liam and Colin, who had been putting the extra leaf in the dining room table, joined them in the kitchen. Both men walked straight over to the plate of cookies and helped themselves to a couple.

"If you guys eat all of the cookies today, I'm not making more. I am officially done baking, and I won't feel a bit sorry for you if you don't have any left for tomorrow," Emma scolded.

"Nil ní níos géire ná teanga mná," Colin said as he looked at Liam, and the two of them grinned mischievously.

"What did you say? Liam, what did Colin say about me?" Emma questioned.

"I said, 'There's nothin' sharper than a woman's tongue,'" Colin translated with a grin.

"Well, you can both remember my sharp tongue tomorrow when you're wondering where all of the cookies have gone, and you realize you have no one to blame but yourselves." Emma smirked.

"Can't help it. They're delicious," Liam mumbled through the cookie in his mouth.

"Did ya help make 'em, love?" Colin asked Sadie as he draped his arm around her shoulders.

"No, I was too busy loading the dishwasher and rolling out the dough for the noodles. I can't take credit for the cookies." Her face lit up like a lightbulb the moment Colin was near.

"She did make two pecan pies, though, and the rumor is they're your favorite." Emma smiled at Colin.

"Ah, the rumor is true. I do love a good pecan pie. Thanks for makin' them, *mo ghrá*." Colin kissed Sadie on the lips after explaining that the words meant 'my love' in English.

Emma truly believed Sadie was blind if she couldn't see how crazy that man was about her.

"I can finish cleaning up here if you two lovebirds want to leave and spend some time alone," Emma giggled as they came up for air.

"Yeah, you guys should go. Enjoy your time together. I'll help Emma finish cleaning up in here." Liam patted Colin on the back before draping his arm over his wife's shoulder.

"A'right. Let's be on our way, *mo stór*. That means 'my treasure,' in case ya haven't learned that one yet," Colin explained to Sadie as he grabbed her hand, helped her into her coat, and waved goodbye to Liam and Emma.

"You're sweet." Sadie flushed at the new name as she followed Colin out the door.

"They are so good together. I'm not the only one who sees

that, am I? He really does care for her, doesn't he?" Emma knew she wasn't wrong about the way Colin felt for Sadie.

"Of course he does. He cares for her deeply. I told you to stop worrying," Liam replied.

"I can't. She's my best friend." Emma shrugged.

"Your faithful, caring heart is what I love the most about you." Liam planted a kiss on the top of Emma's head.

"You know, that Gaelic stuff is pretty sexy. You always seem to be able to translate what Colin is saying." Emma smiled at her husband.

"Yeah, of course I know what he's saying. My parents are Irish too, remember?" Liam's eyes twinkled mischievously.

"But you never speak the language. Did you learn it when you were young?" She couldn't believe she'd never asked Liam about it before.

"We did. Leslie and I are both fluent Gaelic speakers, although I'm kind of rusty since I don't use it much. My parents used to speak it a lot, especially when they were yelling at one of us." He laughed.

"Say something to me." Emma wrapped her arms around his neck. She was amazed that she continued to learn new things about her husband every day.

"Tá tú mo domhan," Liam said quietly.

Emma had no idea what the words meant, but her heart melted a bit at the lyrical sounds.

"What did you say?"

"I said, 'You are my world'," Liam translated as he pulled Emma closer.

"And you are mine," she whispered back.

SEVEN

Sadie and Emma bustled around the kitchen the following day, trying to get everything prepared before the guests arrived. Liam and Colin were entertaining the girls in the living room, and Emma heard the sounds of the Thanksgiving Day Parade coming from the television.

"They're going to be here any minute," Sadie said nervously as she mashed the potatoes.

"Yes, they are. And they're going to love you," Emma encouraged her nervous friend.

"I certainly hope so, but you have to promise you'll help me if it all goes downhill. If I say something stupid, you have to jump in."

"Don't worry. First of all, you're not going to say anything stupid. You're one of the smartest people I know. Second of all, if you do slip and say something silly, I promise to rescue you."

Sadie jumped as the doorbell rang. "Oh no! It's them." She grimaced.

"Liam will answer the door. Just breathe and pull yourself together. They're only people, after all."

"They're not only people, Em. They're the parents of the man I love." Sadie smoothed her hair and checked her makeup in the microwave door.

Emma heard voices intermingling in the hallway, and she knew everyone had arrived. She grabbed Sadie's clammy hand and pulled her along to greet their guests.

"Emma, my dear, you look beautiful as always." Eliza, Liam's mother, pulled her into a giant hug the minute Emma rounded the corner.

"I'm so happy you all could come. Sadie and I have been cooking for days. It's been such fun for me." Emma grinned at her wonderful mother-in-law.

"Sadie, it's so nice to see you again." Eliza embraced Sadie, who looked as if she might faint any second. "You look a little green around the gills, Sadie dear. Are you nervous about meeting Colin's parents?"

Eliza was a very intuitive woman. She'd hit the nail directly on the head.

"I am, but please don't tell them," Sadie answered quietly.

"I wouldn't dream of it. But you needn't be nervous. Colin has been talking about you for months. You have nothing to worry about. Dylan and Fionnula are pure gems."

While Sadie received a pep talk from Eliza, Emma greeted Leslie, Liam's sister, and Tom, her husband. She hadn't seen them since her wedding, but they spoke on the phone regularly. Amber and Alicia, their daughters, had already run into the living room and found the girls. There were squeals of delight as the cousins were reunited.

Duncan, Liam's father, gave Emma a giant bear hug and introduced her to his brother and sister-in-law. "Dylan and Fionnula, I'd like you to meet my other daughter. This is Liam's wife, Emma."

"Emma, we've heard so much about ya." Dylan, who was

nearly an exact replica of his brother, hugged Emma. No wonder Liam and Colin looked so much alike; their fathers could also be twins. The O'Reilly genes were strong.

"Darlin' girl, let me hug ya," Fionnula said in her lilting, melodic voice.

"I'm so pleased you could be with us today. The house feels alive with all of the family here." Having so many people to share her life made Emma's heart full. Her parents would have been happy to see that all these wonderful folks loved her and her girls so much.

"Ma, Da, I'd like ya to meet someone," Colin cut in, then led his parents to where Sadie was standing. "This is Sadie Ross, the girl I been tellin' ya about."

"Sadie, my darlin', you are just as lovely as my boy said ya were." Fionnula pulled Sadie into a warm hug, and Emma almost heard her best friend breathe a huge sigh of relief.

"Thank you, Mrs. O'Reilly," Sadie replied. "I'm so happy to finally get the chance to meet you."

"Oh goodness, dear girl, don't be callin' me Mrs. O'Reilly. It makes me think of my mother-in-law, God rest her soul. Just call me Fionnula, or Fionn, like everyone else does." She laughed, a merry, musical sound, and hugged Sadie again.

"How did a pretty girl like yourself get hooked up with an ugly thing like my son? He's got a face like a blind cobbler's thumb," Dylan said with a grin.

"Come on, Da. Don't humiliate me in front of my girl," Colin chided as his cheeks flushed red with embarrassment.

"Your son is pretty fantastic, if you ask me, sir." Sadie smiled as Dylan hugged her tightly.

"He is for sure," Dylan admitted.

About that time, Sadie's parents, Victoria and Amos, arrived. The rounds of introductions began all over again. From the look on Colin's face when she introduced them,

Emma gathered that he was just as nervous about meeting her parents as she'd been about meeting his. Needless to say, neither of them had anything to worry about. The two of them were a perfect match, and everyone around could see it.

"Please, everyone come in and sit. No need to stand around all day."

With a wave Emma led them into the dining room. She and Sadie had painstakingly decorated the table, and Emma insisted upon using her mother's best china dishes. It was a small way of incorporating her parents into the meal. Emma always missed them dreadfully around the holidays, and this year was no exception. Having a house full of family to share the day gave her more warmth and love than she'd had in years.

Once they were all seated around the table, each person would take a moment to give thanks for something.

"I'll begin," Liam volunteered. "I'm thankful for my beautiful wife, and my four wonderful daughters. I never thought I would have so many blessings in my life, but I'm so grateful that I do. We've been through a lot the past couple of years, and there were a few times when I thought I'd lost Emma for good, but she always came back to me." He looked lovingly at his wife as he spoke.

"Thanks for making me cry in front of everyone, honey." Emma smiled through her tears. "I'll go next. I'm thankful for my husband, and my daughters, and my best friend, and my large extended family. I'm grateful that you're all here with us today. There was a time in my life that I was completely closed off. When I lost my parents, I believed I would never really feel loved again. I am so happy that I was wrong, and that I have all of you wonderful people in my life."

Liam squeezed her hand beneath the table, the girls

smiled happily at their mother, and everyone around the table nodded in understanding.

"I'm thankful for Mama and Daddy," Rose said simply when her turn came.

"I'm thankful for my sisters and my cousins," Dahlia continued with a wide grin.

"I'm thankful for clothes, and ballet class, and my friends. And I'm thankful for my family." Lily smiled.

They continued around the table, each person giving thanks for their blessings. It was a beautiful moment, and the love within the room was palpable. Emma could almost see her parents smiling down on her.

"I'll go next." Colin cleared his throat and rose from his chair. "When I came to America, I never intended to stay. I came to help out with that awful mess with Emma, and I always figured I'd leave when it was resolved. But I met this lovely woman, and she stole my heart."

Colin shifted from foot to foot, and he looked very nervous. Sadie squirmed in her chair, obviously uncomfortable with so many eyes upon the two of them.

He continued, "I've spent the last two years gettin' to know her, and every day I admire her more. She's shown me what true beauty looks like—the kind of beauty that isn't only skin deep. She has the biggest, kindest heart of any woman I've ever known, and her quick wit and sharp mind keep a mate like me on my toes."

Colin stopped speaking and cleared his throat again. The room was so silent you could have heard a pin drop. Everyone was waiting to hear what he would say next.

Colin reached into his pocket and pulled out a small box. He dropped to his knee beside the table and turned his body toward Sadie. She gasped loudly.

"Sadie, *mo ghrá*, I feel like I've loved ya since I laid eyes on ya. I canna go back to Ireland until I get an answer. *An bpós-faidh tú mé?*" Colin's voice shook with emotion as he spoke.

No one in the room made a sound.

"Did you just ask what I think you asked?" Sadie blinked in wonder.

"I asked ya to be my wife. I love ya, *mo ghrá*."

"Oh, Colin, yes, yes, yes! Oh, a hundred times yes!" Sadie threw herself into Colin's arms and everyone burst into a round of applause as the couple kissed each other.

"Enough snoggin'," Dylan teased his son, but the lovebirds were so engrossed in each other that they paid no attention.

"Leave the boy alone, Dylan," Fionnula chided her husband.

"Well, I'm glad your answer was yes, love. I have somethin' for ya." Colin opened the box and pulled out a ring. "This ring has been in Ma's family for over a hundred years." He slipped the sparkling diamond onto Sadie's finger as tears ran down her face.

"It's beautiful. I've never seen anything like it before. What does the symbol around the diamond mean?" Sadie stared in wonder at the ring on her hand.

"It's a Claddagh ring, *mo ghrá*. The clasped hands stand for friendship, which is very important in a marriage. The heart represents love, and I promise to love ya until the day I die. The crown stands for loyalty. I'll be yours faithfully until the end of time. I've placed it on your left finger facing away from you. That signifies that we're engaged. Once we're married, you'll turn it in to face ya, and everyone will know you're my wife," Colin explained the lovely tradition.

"Oh, Colin, I'm so happy." Sadie hugged him tightly. "I was terrified that you would leave and I'd never see you again."

"Never see ya again? *Mo ghrá*, I would surely die if I never saw you again." Colin brushed the tears from Sadie's cheeks.

"But Colin, you have to go back to Ireland in two days. What will we do? Please tell me you have a plan, because I can't be without you," Sadie finally admitted.

"I do have to go back to Ireland. There's no gettin' around that. I have plans to make if I'm gonna live in America with ya," Colin answered.

"You're going to move here with me? You would do that?" Sadie asked in wonder.

"Of course I would. Your life is here, and my life is wherever you are, *mo ghrá*. But I do have one request."

"Name it."

"I've always wanted to get married in Cloghan Castle. It's about twenty miles outside of my hometown of Galway City. It was built in 1239, and 'tis lovely. Will ya marry me there?"

"Will I marry you in an ancient Irish castle?" Sadie's eyes grew bigger than our dinner plates as she squealed and clapped her hands wildly. "That would be like a beautiful dream come true. I would marry you in a run-down barn if you asked me to—as long as we were together at the end of it." Sadie laughed and the rest of the table cheered.

"So when's the big day?" Liam prodded.

"Yes, we have so much to plan. And you leave to go back in two days! What are we going to do?" Sadie's brow furrowed and she bit her lower lip, obviously worried as to how they were going to pull off wedding plans across the ocean.

"I wouldn't fret too much. Your husband-to-be has been planning this for months. Why do you think we're here?" Duncan asked with a sly grin.

"You all knew about this?" Sadie looked around the table.

"Everyone knew except for you and Emma," Liam admitted.

"You knew and you didn't tell me?" Emma couldn't believe Liam had kept such a huge secret from her.

"I couldn't tell you. You and Sadie can practically read each other's minds. If you knew, she would know too, and the surprise was too good to spoil. The only way to keep it from her was to keep it from you as well. Forgive me?" Liam kissed Emma's hand.

Emma was far too happy for Sadie to be upset about anything. "For this? Yes. How could I not forgive you?"

"So tell everyone what you have planned, Colin. I can't wait to see the look on my daughter's face when she hears what you've concocted." Victoria's face shone with the same excitement as her daughter's.

"Well, love, this is what I've come up with. Anything you don't like, just say so," Colin began.

"I can't believe you've been making plans while I've been busy worrying," Sadie said with a shake of her head. "Tell me all about it."

"Well, I have to go back to Ireland to tie up some loose ends, but I was thinkin' that a Valentine's Day wedding in a castle would be pretty magical. Do ya agree?"

"Valentine's Day? Oh, Colin, it's perfect!" Sadie clapped her hands together in glee.

"I'm glad ya said so, since I already made the reservations at the castle." He grinned sheepishly.

"You really have thought of everything, haven't you?" Sadie laughed.

"*Mo stór*, I been thinkin' of makin' ya my wife since I first saw ya. I've been plannin' it for months. All ya have to do now is find the perfect dress." Colin smiled.

Emma couldn't have been happier for Sadie. It seemed that Colin was just as romantic as Liam.

"I suppose it's a good thing I said yes, then, isn't it?" Sadie giggled.

"'Tis a grand thing, indeed," Colin agreed. "And everyone at this table will be travelin' to Ireland for our wedding. The plans have been made, and the tickets have already been bought."

"You are an amazing man. You've made me the happiest woman alive, Colin." Sadie pressed her lips to his and everyone cheered again.

"Slainté!" Liam said as he raised his glass in a toast.

"Slainté!" everyone echoed.

EIGHT

"Looks like you're almost a free man, Smith." Tony, the crooked prison guard who was disguised as an ER nurse, glanced around furtively as he quickly wheeled Xavier to the curb outside of the hospital. Tony had changed into the contraband nurse's scrubs in the utility closet. Another one of Xavier's contacts, John, just happened to be an ER nurse, and he had aided Tony and Xavier in the switch. John was hiding out in the utility closet until he and Tony switched back once Xavier was safe and sound.

Unfortunately for Tony, he was also sporting a split lip, and what promised to be a whopper of a black eye. They'd needed to make it look good, after all. If Tony had any hope of not landing in prison himself, it had to appear that he'd tried to stop Xavier from escaping. It was all going according to plan.

"I'm nearly free indeed, thanks to you. My man should be here any moment, and you'll be paid well." Xavier shifted in the wheelchair and winced from the pain that originated just below his left shoulder.

Durant's strike had been successful, and although the

wound was painful, it had been well worth it. He'd been transported to the ER under the watchful eyes of Tony, who had put on the nurse's scrubs to ensure Xavier's getaway. The sleek black Mercedes driven by Billy, another one of Xavier's longtime associates, pulled up in the hospital pickup lane as they'd arranged.

"Xavier, my man." Billy jumped out of the car, opened the passenger side door, and stood back as Tony helped Xavier inside.

"Pay the man, Billy," Xavier commanded.

"Sure thing, boss." Billy handed Tony a wad of cash.

Xavier chuckled as the guard's eyes widened greedily. "Don't forget to give John his share when you give him his scrubs back."

"I'll see to it," Tony mumbled.

"Let's get out of here before we attract too much attention," Xavier barked.

Billy nodded quickly, patted Tony on the back, shut the passenger door, jumped behind the wheel, and sped out of town.

"Billy, it is good to see you again." Xavier exhaled loudly once he knew they were out of harm's way.

Everything had gone exactly according to plan, and he was a free man.

"So where am I taking you?" Billy asked.

"Beckland," Xavier answered without hesitation.

"There's nothing in Beckland. What could you possibly want with that place?"

"Beckland is just the starting point. It's where the adventure really begins. Take me there, and stop asking so many questions."

"Sure thing. Whatever you say, boss," Billy conceded.

An hour and a half later, after Xavier left Billy at the bus station, he situated himself behind the wheel of the

Mercedes. He hadn't driven for two years, and feeling the powerful car beneath his body was a rush. He knew he should just jump on the highway and drive away to freedom, but he couldn't. He was so close to Emma, and he had to see her. The pull was too strong for him to resist. He needed to get one small glimpse of her to keep him going until they were together again.

He drove across town and pulled up in front of her house. He remembered the last time he was there, the night he'd almost made her his for good. If they hadn't been interrupted by Liam, he and Emma would be living happily ever after somewhere far away from there. That little glitch in his plan was going to be remedied very soon.

He pulled the car into a parking spot across the street from Morning Glory. He fumbled quickly in the glove compartment, grabbed the black knitted skull cap and dark sunglasses, and put them on. It wasn't much of a disguise, but it would have to do. Besides, he looked quite different from the last time Emma had seen him. He had shaved his head, so he was completely bald. He'd also increased the bulk of his body to more than twice the size he'd been before. She wouldn't recognize him unless she got a good look at him, and that wasn't going to happen.

Xavier exited the car and sat on the bench that conveniently looked through the front windows of Morning Glory. He sucked in his breath when he saw her. She looked more beautiful than he'd remembered, her smile lighting up the room. Her lovely strawberry waves cascaded down her back, and he wanted to reach out and feel the softness. He longed to caress her perfect, pale skin and hear her warm laughter. He needed to get closer.

Xavier glanced across the street and noticed there was another bench right outside the front door of the coffee shop. If he sat there, he might be able to hear her voice when the door opened. It would be a good place to sit and listen. It was risky, but most rewarding things were.

He walked quickly across the road and slumped on the bench, wincing at the pain in his shoulder. Pulling out a book, he pretended to read as he shivered in the cold November air. He decided he would only sit there for a few minutes, and then he would be on his way; he just needed to hear her voice to hold him over a little while longer.

Xavier sat on that bench for two hours, listening to the sweet, hypnotic sound of Emma talking to her customers every time the front door opened. Not only had he gotten to see and hear her, but he'd also gained some useful information in the process. He'd learned that Emma and her family would be heading to Galway, Ireland, to celebrate a Valentine's Day wedding in Cloghan Castle. Emma's best friend was marrying Liam's cousin, and the whole family would be there.

Even more importantly, he learned that they would all be distracted with the planning of the event. None of them would have time to give him a second thought. It was perfect.

A huge smile broke out on Xavier's face as he realized that everything was finally falling into place. For once, the universe was conspiring to give him exactly what he wanted. He knew just what he was going to do, and he was more certain than ever that it was going to work exactly the way he wanted it to.

He took one last, lingering look at Emma before tearing himself away from the front of the coffee shop, walking across the street, and gingerly climbing inside of the Mercedes. Drumming his fingers on the steering wheel, he contemplated the future. He wanted nothing more than to take Emma with him at that very moment, and he had to fight the impulse to do exactly that. It wasn't part of his strategy, and he had to remember the plan.

"Stick to the rules, Xavier. It's the only way to take care of things once and for all," he murmured to himself.

Although his heart was begging to be close to Emma, his head won out in the end. He knew that in order to make Emma his for a lifetime, he must be patient. Everything was laid out, and he had to stick to the schedule. It would take every bit of the three months he'd allowed himself to make it happen. There was the business of obtaining a new identity for the necessary travel documents, lining up his finances, and calling in favors from his contacts around the world. What he planned to do was risky, time-consuming, and very expensive.

He turned the key in the ignition, blew a kiss in Emma's direction, and sped out of Beckland.

"Emma, my love, we will meet again very soon."

PART TWO
FEBRUARY

Ireland
*"The future is not set, there is no fate but what we make for
ourselves."* –Irish Proverb

NINE

Emma's stomach churned in excitement and anticipation as the airplane made its initial descent into the awaiting Shannon Airport. They'd been traveling for what seemed like days, when in reality it was only around six and a half hours. The group had flown from Columbus to New Jersey, then traveled nonstop to Shannon.

The flight had been smooth, but Emma's daughters were cranky, and she was at her wit's end trying to keep squirmy, busy little Daisy entertained. The other three girls had slept most of the way, but Emma could tell they were in a hurry to get off the plane as well.

"We're almost there, girls. Just a few more minutes and we'll be in Ireland." Emma said the words for her daughters' benefit as well as her own.

"My butt is numb, Mama," Rose complained.

"Mine is, too. You've been a very good girl, though, and I appreciate it." Emma squeezed Rose's hand while Daisy pulled her mother's hair.

"Daddy, is this where you were born?" Dahlia asked Liam.

"No, sweetie, I was born in America. But my parents were

both born in Ireland. I've been back to visit several times, though, and I know you girls are going to love it," he answered.

"I've heard people talk about coming back to the land of their ancestors and feeling as if they belong there. Did that happen to you?" Emma glanced at Liam, brows raised, before returning her attention to Daisy.

"Actually, yes, it did. I would have never believed in such a phenomenon if I hadn't experienced it. Honestly, I'll never forget the first time I saw Ireland for myself. It was like coming home to a place that I'd never been before. It was unsettling and comforting all at the same time." Liam smiled wistfully.

"My parents never really talked about where our ancestors came from. Our family has been in Ohio for as long as anyone can remember. Someday I think I'd like to know more." Emma wondered where her own family tree might find its roots.

"Well, honey, given your hair color and pale skin, I'm willing to bet you have an Irish connection somewhere down the line. We'll see if the land calls to you like it did to me." Liam grinned mysteriously.

"Yeah, maybe it will." Emma smiled in answer.

The group stowed their belongings and prepared for landing. A few minutes later, Liam, Sadie, and Emma ushered four very exhausted little girls through the airport. After making it through customs, they headed to baggage claim, where Colin was supposed to meet them.

"I'll bet you can't wait to see Colin." Emma smiled at Sadie as they grabbed the last of their bags from the conveyor belt.

"Oh my goodness, Em, I am going to kiss that man so hard when I see him! I know it's only been a couple of months since he left, but it seems like years. I can't believe I'm marrying him in two days," Sadie gushed excitedly.

"Sadie!"

Every head turned as Colin's voice called from across the airport. Sadie dropped her bags at her feet. Like a shot fired out of a cannon, she sprinted toward him, flinging herself into his arms and smothering him with a thousand kisses.

Emma was happy to see the couple together once again. The past months had been hard on her friend. She'd hated being so far away from the man she loved. From the look of things, Colin felt the same way.

Liam grabbed Sadie's abandoned bags from the ground and loaded them onto the luggage cart. Colin approached and hugged them before helping Liam wheel the cart outside to the parking area. Sadie grabbed Daisy and carried her while Emma corralled the other three girls, leading them to the parking garage. Everyone piled into Colin's vehicle, a fifteen-passenger van that he'd rented so he could transport the large group.

Both Liam's and Sadie's parents were flying in the following day, and Emma couldn't wait until the entire gang arrived. The Valentine's Day wedding was going to be such a joyful celebration.

"How far do we have to drive until we get there?" Lily questioned with a sigh. The girls were exhausted, and they wanted nothing more than to be able to move about freely.

"'Tis only a little over an hour, Lily. I promise we'll be there soon," Colin answered. "You should take a look out your window, darlin'. You're about to see some of the prettiest scenery on Earth. And you're gonna love Galway. 'Tis the cultural center of Ireland."

Looking out the window, Emma took in the view around her with a kind of reverent awe. Colin was right. She'd never seen anywhere more green, lush, or magical. Everywhere she looked was like a picture-perfect postcard. Rolling verdant hills dotted with grazing sheep greeted her gaze as she peered out the window.

Narrow roads lined with ancient stone walls caused her breath to catch. The dancing grasses and gray, gloomy clouds spoke to Emma on a deep level. It was almost too much to take in. Her eyes filled with tears and her heart pounded inside of her chest. She felt a primal, almost surreal sense of belonging in the strange and wonderful place. It made her wonder if her roots had indeed found their start on the Emerald Isle.

"Are you all right, Emma?" Liam leaned toward her and whispered.

Emma tried hard to find the words to convey the unexplainable feelings. "I am. This place is just so... well... magical is the only word that even comes close, but that is such an inadequate description. I feel very emotional, and I don't know why."

"I understand completely. I told you, it's exactly how I felt the first time I was here. There's really no place else like it." He patted her leg and clasped her hand inside of his.

"I had no idea it would be so moving. As crazy as it sounds, it's almost as if the land is speaking to me," Emma said quietly as she gazed out the window and tried to drink it all in.

The vehicle grew quiet as everyone surveyed the wonder around them. Daisy had dropped off to sleep almost as soon as the van began moving, and the older girls seemed to be just as awestruck by the landscape as their mother.

Before long, Colin announced their arrival. He turned down a winding driveway, and Emma smiled as Dylan and Fionnula's lovely stone house came into view.

"Oh, Colin, it looks just like something out of a fairy tale." Emma smiled.

"Ma will be happy to hear that ya think so. She told me

when I was a boy that the house was built by the faeries. I've never been quite sure if it was a tale or not," Colin replied with a grin.

"It was so kind of your parents to put us all up for the night. We're quite the motley crew, and I'm not sure if she knows what she's gotten herself into." Emma laughed.

"Ma and Da wouldn't have it any other way. You're family. In Ireland, family doesn't spend the night in a hotel." Colin parked the van and turned the key in the ignition. "Besides, it's only for tonight. Tomorrow, we'll all be sleepin' in a castle."

"My friends were so jealous when I told them I was going to a castle." Dahlia smiled broadly.

"Mine, too. They started calling me Princess Lily. I sort of liked it," Lily giggled.

"I can't wait to wear my pretty dress, Mama," Rose said.

"It's going to be wonderful, isn't it, girls?" Emma smiled at her daughters as they went inside.

They were all greeted with hugs and kisses from Dylan and Fionnula, who led them upstairs into the rooms they would occupy for the night. Colin had whisked Sadie away somewhere, and Emma couldn't help but smile at their obviously happy reunion. She knew how she would feel if she and Liam had been separated for that long, and she was sure they were making up for lost time.

"Emma, how about if I take the girls downstairs for a snack and some playtime while you catch your breath for a few minutes?" Fionnula asked.

"I appreciate it, but I don't want you to go to any extra trouble. We've already bombarded your home for the night."

"Darlin', 'tisn't a bit of trouble. Your dear girls are just lovely, and I want to spend some time gettin' to know 'em better. I'm always surrounded by men, so 'twill be a refreshin' change. Besides, after bein' on a plane for that many hours with four children, ya deserve a bit o' peace and quiet."

"You are a gem." Emma sighed as she hugged the kind woman. "I am exhausted. I'll happily take a few moments to collect my thoughts and breathe. Thank you."

"Thanks, Aunt Fionn," Liam replied.

"Take your time. Once you're rested, you might like to explore Galway a bit." Fionnula smiled as she led the girls away and shut the door behind her.

Emma breathed a huge sigh of relief and collapsed on the nearby bed. Lying down was probably a mistake, seeing as how she wouldn't want to get up again, but she couldn't help it. Between the long, tiring flight and the huge time change, she needed a few moments to rest. She patted the bed beside her, and Liam placed his weary body next to his wife's.

"I can't believe we're really here," Emma said in wonder. "We've been planning it for a couple of months, but somehow I didn't believe it would actually happen. It feels like a dream, but it's real, isn't it? Sadie is getting married in two days, in a castle in Ireland, and we're all a part of it."

"It certainly is real. It makes me wish we had done something this special for our wedding. If only I could have given all of this to you."

"Liam, don't think for one second that our wedding wasn't special. It was the most magical, perfect day of my life." She took his face in her hands and locked her eyes onto his.

"I know, but it certainly wasn't in a castle. You should have had a wedding fit for a queen. You deserve it."

"Where we got married isn't important. Liam, you saved my life the day you walked into my coffee shop, and you have continued to save it over and over again every single day. The ceremony was just the beginning, and I wouldn't trade that moment for a thousand weddings in a thousand castles.

That was the day our family became complete, and in my eyes, it was perfect."

"You're perfect. I'm lucky you agreed to be my wife." He traced his fingertip over her cheek and her body tingled.

"I'm the lucky one, Liam."

Emma covered his lips with hers, and as her heart began to beat more quickly, she realized that she wasn't tired anymore.

TEN

Emma slept like a rock that night, snuggled next to Liam, with Daisy's tiny body wedged in between them. Lily, Rose, and Dahlia slept soundly in the room next door. They'd run on adrenaline for the remainder of the day, but when nighttime settled in, they'd all collapsed from exhaustion.

The faint light of morning trickled its way in through the lacy curtains on the windows, and Emma's eyes fluttered open. She smiled, still not quite able to believe that she was waking up in Ireland. It was surreal to think that later that afternoon they would all head to Cloghan Castle to spend the night. Emma was beyond thrilled that her best friend would be marrying the man of her dreams in just twenty-four hours.

She glanced at her sleeping baby, whose tiny fists clutched Liam's shirt tightly. The two of them resting peacefully made her heart happy. There was a time, not too long ago, that Emma believed happiness had been forever stolen from her. Xavier Smith had tried twice to destroy her life. He'd attempted to rip her from the arms of her husband and children, but those days were over.

Good had triumphed over evil, and love had won. Emma's heart beat a little faster as she prayed that her streak of good luck would continue. Right after Thanksgiving, there had been a prison break at the Ohio State Penitentiary, and she'd immediately panicked when she'd heard about it on the news. She'd been convinced that Xavier was a part of it. Most of the pertinent details had been kept under wraps, because a crooked guard was suspected in helping with the escape, although nothing had ever been proven.

She'd asked Liam if she should be worried. He'd assured her that she was safe, so she hadn't asked any more questions. Emma was finally getting back to her normal life, and she couldn't bear to think that something might happen to her again. In order to make it through each day, Emma had to believe that what Liam told her was true. She wasn't in danger. Nearly three months later, she believed he'd been right. Nothing bad was going to happen to them again.

Thinking of what she'd been through still haunted her if she dwelled on it too long. In two short years, Emma's family had endured more trials and heartache than most people experienced over a lifetime. She was convinced that there was nothing left for them but joy. She refused to believe anything else. If she wanted to continue healing, she *couldn't* believe anything else.

Together, she and Liam had chased away the darkness, and she was grateful to be basking in the light. Every day, she walked farther away from the nightmare of a madman's world.

As she lay in bed, contemplating whether or not she should move and disrupt the stillness, she thought about her plans for the day. Liam and Colin were entertaining the girls while she and Sadie ventured into Galway City for a little pre-wedding pampering. They had manicures and pedicures scheduled for later that morning, and Emma couldn't wait to have a bit of girl time with her best friend. As happy as she was for Sadie and Colin, Emma couldn't help but be aware that life as she knew it was about to change.

For as long as Emma could remember, she and the girls had been the center of Sadie's world. Her best friend had devoted her whole life to Emma's family, and Emma had leaned on Sadie heavily over the years. Although Sadie would always remain Emma's closest friend, and she would continue to be there for them, everything would be different after the wedding. Before long, Sadie would be a wife. The center of her world would shift from Emma's family to her own.

It wasn't that Emma was jealous. She just needed to come to terms with the fact that Sadie would never be devoted to her in quite the same way again. As much as Emma hated change, she had to admit that it was time for Sadie to begin her own journey. She'd selfishly had her best friend's undivided attention for a long time, and that spot would soon belong to Colin, as it should. Sadie deserved exactly what Emma had found with Liam.

Emma shifted her weight and Daisy made a sound, but remained asleep. Liam rolled over and mumbled something indiscernible. She didn't want to wake them, but she was ready to begin the day.

Sliding quietly out of bed, she padded across the beautiful hardwood floor and into the adjoining bathroom. Closing the door behind her, she took a quick shower, threw on her clothes, applied minimal makeup, and quietly slipped out the door.

Emma walked down the hallway and peeked through the half-open door into the room where her other girls were sleeping. They were resting quietly and looked just like angels. She pulled the door shut without a sound and headed downstairs.

Fionnula was already awake, humming in the kitchen while she prepared a large traditional Irish breakfast. Emma watched the woman work her magic, moving quickly across the kitchen floor like some sort of automated breakfast-making machine. Fionnula cooked up bacon and sausages, eggs, potatoes, and a strange-looking dish that Emma thought might be black pudding.

She'd done some research before she'd left Ohio, so Emma knew a few of the traditional foods that might be served while they were in Ireland. Although she was game for almost anything, she had to admit that she was not too eager to sample the black pudding. From the expert way Fionnula handled food preparation, though, Emma had a feeling the older woman was a master chef. Perhaps she could make even that dish palatable.

"Morning, darlin' girl." Fionnula turned and smiled at Emma as she pulled a loaf of soda bread out of the oven. "I hope ya slept sound."

"Oh yes, I slept like a rock. I don't remember a thing after my head hit the pillow."

"I knew you'd be needin' a good night's rest after that long flight. Are your lil' angels still asleep?"

"Yes, it seems I was the only one ready to begin the day. What time is it anyway?" Emma still hadn't adjusted to the time change, and she thought she might be asking what time it was until she returned to Ohio.

"It's only six o'clock. I didn't think you'd be up for a couple of hours yet. Me, I'm an early riser. Always have been. So is my Dylan, although today he's still sleepin'. I figured I'd get a head start on the cookin'." Fionnula turned the sausages in the pan without looking. "That husband o' mine is always starvin' when he wakes."

"It smells amazing in here. Do you cook like this every

morning?" Emma was astounded at how much food Fionnula had prepared.

"Goodness no, child. Hearty breakfasts are usually reserved for the weekends or special occasions. But havin' family here to share it with seemed like a pretty special occasion to me." Fionnula smiled as she scrambled the eggs.

"Well it looks delicious. I don't know when the rest of the crew will wake up, though. I figured I'd let them sleep as long as they wanted. Sadie and I are heading into town as soon as she gets up and around. The men are in charge of the girls today." Emma seated herself at the large kitchen table as Fionnula handed her a mug of steaming hot tea.

Emma took a sip and sighed with pleasure. "Thank you, Fionn."

"You're welcome, darlin'," the older woman replied as she sat down next to Emma with her own mug.

"Looks like the women are the only ones up and about this morning." Sadie's voice drifted into the peaceful silence of the kitchen.

"Morning, Sadie." Emma patted the seat on the other side of her and Sadie sat down.

"I'll grab you some tea, love." Fionnula grinned at her soon-to-be daughter-in-law.

"I can get it. Please don't trouble yourself." Sadie, who still seemed a bit nervous around Fionnula, started to stand.

"'Tis no trouble at all." Fionnula urged Sadie to sit as she grabbed another mug and filled it. She returned to the table, handed it to Sadie, who whispered her thanks, and took a seat.

"This is nice." Emma smiled at the women seated next to her. "I'm not used to lazy mornings. Usually it's a mad dash getting kids ready for school and myself ready for work."

"I don't know how you do it, Emma. I had a hard time gettin' myself out of the house when Colin was a boy, and there was only one of him. I can't imagine four!" Fionnula shook her head in wonder.

Sadie patted Emma's hand and smiled at her. "Emma is Superwoman. I came to that conclusion years ago."

"I'm thinkin' she must be." Fionnula bobbed her head in agreement.

"Nonsense. I just do what needs done," Emma argued, uncomfortable at having the attention focused on her.

"What about you, darlin' girl? Do ya think you and my son will be havin' any children?" Fionnula's gaze fell upon Sadie, and Emma noticed her friend's cheeks turn an adorable shade of pink.

Sadie cleared her throat nervously. "Well, I know we would both like to."

"I'm certainly hopin' so. I was only blessed with one child, and I always dreamed of havin' a houseful. Maybe I'll still get 'em." Fionnula grinned widely.

"You just might." Sadie smiled broadly, looking completely comfortable for the first time with her future mother-in-law.

"So you two are headed into town for a day of pamperin'?" Fionnula finished her tea.

"We are. We're off for a little pre-wedding celebration," Emma answered.

She thought that perhaps they should invite Fionnula to go along with them. It was probably bad manners not to include their hostess.

Sadie must have had the same thought, because she glanced Emma's way and said, "Fionnula, would you like to come with us? I'm sure we could get you an appointment, too."

"Nonsense! You girls go enjoy your day. I've got plenty to do around here before we head to Cloghan Castle later on. Besides, those men might need a little help lookin' after the girls. And even if they don't, I'd love to spend some more time with 'em. I can't seem to get enough." She smiled brightly.

"If you're sure…," Emma hedged.

"I'm more than sure. You should grab a bite to eat and take off before everyone wakes up and wants your attention." Fionnula rose from the table, grabbed two plates, piled them full of food, and served breakfast to Sadie and Emma.

The ladies gobbled up Fionnula's delicious food, and they even tried the black pudding. It wasn't nearly as dreadful as Emma had imagined it to be, but she couldn't fathom eating it very often. When they finished, Emma and Sadie helped Fionnula wash the dishes, ignoring her instructions that she didn't want them to lift a finger.

"I've drawn ya a map of how to get into town. It's not far at all, and 'tis difficult to get lost, but here it is, just in case." Fionnula handed Emma a folded slip of paper. "Are ya sure ya don't want to use the car?"

"It's a lovely morning, and Colin said it's less than half a mile into town. I think we would enjoy the walk," Sadie replied.

"Besides, we've never driven on the wrong side of the street, so I'm guessing that could end badly. We'd better stick to walking." Emma giggled as she imagined herself crashing Fionnula's car into one of the stone walls alongside the road.

"Well, you ladies have a grand time, and we'll see ya later on."

Sadie and Emma hugged Fionnula goodbye and snuck out of the house before anyone else awoke. It was a cloudy morning, and the fog was fairly thick, but that simply made the surroundings feel even more mystical. Sadie and Emma ambled along the narrow road that led into Galway City, completely mesmerized by the beautiful landscape all around them.

"I can't believe I'm getting married tomorrow, Em," Sadie said quietly.

"It's going to be beautiful. I can't wait to see the castle. And your dress is gorgeous. You're going to look just like a queen when you walk down the aisle to Colin." Emma grabbed Sadie's hand and squeezed it tightly.

"This is really happening, isn't it? All of these weeks, it's felt like I was living inside of a dream, but it's not a dream, is it?" Sadie's eyes glistened with tears.

"No, sweetie, it's real. It's all very real. Tomorrow you'll marry your Prince Charming in a beautiful castle, and you'll begin your life together. There aren't enough words to say how happy I am for you. You're getting everything you've always deserved." Emma continued holding Sadie's hand as they walked along the road.

"I'm so happy, Em. But I'm a little scared, too. Is that normal?" Sadie asked.

"It's completely normal. I was terrified when Liam and I got married. I was afraid of changing the wonderful thing we had together, that marriage would somehow diminish our love, but it was just the opposite. Getting married only made our connection stronger. We became a team. I know he's got my back, no matter what comes our way, and I will do the same for him. It's going to be just as great for you and Colin, I promise," Emma assured her best friend.

"I'll have to trust you on this one. It seems like I've always been on the sidelines, watching you live your life, and now I've been taken off the bench and thrown into a game that I'm not really sure how to play. You've always made marriage and motherhood look so easy. What if I'm bad at it?" Sadie asked tentatively.

"You've never been bad at anything you've ever done. Why should this be any different? Do you want to know why I've succeeded at marriage and motherhood?" Sadie nodded and her hand tightened around Emma's. "Mostly because I've had help. Being a good wife for Liam is easy, and you've helped me be a good mother. I haven't failed, mostly because of you. Now it's my turn to do the same. I'll always be there for you, Sadie."

The women stopped walking and Emma searched in her purse for the small package she'd been carrying around for weeks. She'd planned to give it to her friend on her wedding day, but it seemed to be the right moment.

"I have something for you."

Emma and Sadie veered off the road and leaned against the stone wall that ran alongside it. Emma removed the box from her purse and placed it in Sadie's hand.

"What's this for?" Sadie's eyebrows furrowed.

"It's a gift, for being my best friend." Emma smiled and tried not to let the threatening tears fall. "Open it."

Sadie pulled the white wrapping paper from the small box and opened the lid. She smiled when she saw the tiny silver horseshoe necklace. "It's just like yours."

"Yes it is. Liam gave me my horseshoe necklace the day we got married. He said it's an Irish good luck symbol. The bride is supposed to carry a horseshoe on her wedding day to bring good fortune to the marriage. Since carrying a heavy horseshoe isn't appealing, he bought me a necklace instead. I wanted you to have one, too."

"Emma, it's beautiful. I'll take all of the good fortune I can get." Sadie wiped away her tears and hugged Emma tightly.

"You and Colin don't need luck. Here, let me help you put it on," Emma offered.

"I love the fact that we both have one. Thank you."

"You're welcome. Now enough of this sappiness. Let's go get pampered."

Both women laughed as they resumed their walk into Galway City.

Three hours later, after being manicured and pedicured to their hearts' content, Emma and Sadie left the quaint salon on Eyre Square. Sadie wiggled her French manicured fingertips at her friend and smiled happily. They decided to pop into Esquires Coffee before they headed back to Dylan and Fionnula's house to pack up for their trip to the castle.

Emma grabbed a flat white—similar to a latte, but with less foam and a higher proportion of coffee to milk. The problem with being a coffee shop owner was the fact that Emma knew the difference between all of the drinks, so decision-making was difficult. Sadie kept things simple and just asked for a caffé latte. They thanked the friendly barista for the coffees and continued on their way, taking in the sights as they walked.

Emma was completely mesmerized by the unique, cultured city of Galway. There were street performers all around, and the sounds of traditional Irish folk music danced in the air. The ladies could have listened to it all day, but they had a schedule to keep.

All at once, a strange tingling sensation wrapped its icy fingers around Emma's spine. She had no idea what was wrong, but her happy, joyous afternoon took a quick and sudden shift. Emma glanced at Sadie to see if her friend had noticed anything different, but she appeared to be immersed in the music. Emma turned her head and looked all around, not certain what she might find, but feeling like she needed to do something. The peaceful afternoon had been interrupted, and Emma wanted to know why.

Everyone was enjoying the music, and Emma wondered why no one else felt the thick, black, menacing cloud that had descended over the town. She told herself that she was the only one disturbed by the feeling, so she tried to ignore it. Nothing appeared out of place, and there was no logical reason why Emma should suddenly feel afraid.

But Emma did feel afraid, and no matter how hard she tried to push the feeling away, she couldn't. She rationalized with herself, trying to be mindful of the fact that she was in the most beautiful city in the world. She chided herself for looking for trouble where there was none to be found.

As they left town and headed back to the O'Reilly home, Emma did her best to negate the nagging sensation that something was terribly wrong. It was ridiculous, and she wouldn't spoil Sadie's perfect occasion with her portents of doom.

"Is everything all right, Emma?" Sadie asked.

Emma pushed down her emotions, forced a smile, and grabbed her best friend's hand. "Of course it is. Everything is perfect. Cloghan Castle, here we come."

ELEVEN

The van rolled along the narrow road through the sprawling countryside as the little group made its way to Cloghan Castle. They'd loaded all their bags and gear into the van after Sadie and Emma returned from town, and soon they would arrive at their destination. Cloghan Castle was only a forty-five-minute drive from the O'Reilly home, and Emma had assured her squirmy daughters that they wouldn't have to spend too much time in the van.

They could have driven forever for all Emma cared. Ireland was gorgeous. In each and every direction, there was something new that took her breath away, and she'd come to the conclusion that she'd never tire of taking it all in. Her young daughters, who preferred running through the countryside to viewing it from the van window, looked at things quite differently.

Liam was their personal chauffeur, and Colin and Sadie followed behind them in their car. The rest of the gang would meet at Cloghan later that evening. Dylan and Fionnula were headed to Shannon Airport to pick up Victoria and Amos, as well as Duncan and Eliza. Their plane should be touching down upon Irish soil at any moment.

There would be a grand total of fourteen people spending the night at the castle and attending the wedding the following day. Normally young children weren't allowed on the premises, but somehow Colin had pulled a few strings, ensuring the girls could attend the ceremony. Sadie would have never agreed to get married there if the girls couldn't take part. Dahlia, Rose, and Daisy would have the very important roles of flower girls, and since there weren't any boys in the bunch, Lily would play the part of the ring bearer.

"Look, Emma, there it is," Liam said.

Emma gasped as the magnificent ancient structure came into view. The Norman fortress greeted them with its stone exterior walls, arched doorways, circular turrets, and imposing battlements. Constructed of natural stone from the area, predominately granite, the exterior of the castle was a thing of beauty.

"Oh, Liam, it's amazing," Emma breathed in wonder, knowing words could never fully convey the majesty of the castle.

"I know. I felt the exact same way the first time I saw it. It's been years since I've been here, but it's still one of my favorite spots in all of Ireland. It's truly magical." Liam smiled.

"Mama, did kings and queens live in that castle?" Rose inquired.

"I'm sure a lot of important people have lived there, baby. I was reading that it was built in the 1200s. Can you imagine? There's nothing in the United States that is even close to that old. Just think about all of the stories they would tell if those walls could talk," Emma replied.

Liam pulled the van into one of the parking spaces at the front of the castle, and Colin and Sadie followed suit. They all jumped out of their vehicles, and Emma noticed that her daughters' faces held the same look of wide-eyed wonder that she imagined was on her own.

Standing in front of Cloghan Castle truly felt like being in the middle of a fairy tale. Emma almost expected to see a knight in armor galloping across the yard on his trusty steed. It would be the perfect place for Sadie's wedding.

"Are ya ready to see the inside, love?" Colin asked his soon-to-be wife.

Sadie kissed him deeply, smiled, and nodded excitedly.

"Good. Let's go in and I'll introduce ya to the owners. Ma and Da have known 'em for years," Colin explained.

The group followed Colin's lead and entered the doorway of the magnificent structure. While he chatted animatedly with the castle's proprietors, Emma reveled in the history all around. It was like stepping back in time, hundreds and hundreds of years into the past. She could picture lords and ladies presiding over the household, and she imagined servants hustling and bustling throughout the building, each with an important task to complete.

Ancient stone walls, a medieval chandelier, and even a coat of armor greeted her. The largest staircase she'd ever seen seemed to reach toward the clouds. It beckoned Emma to follow, promising to share the secrets of the ancient feet that had traveled across its surface. When the time came to leave Cloghan Castle, Emma knew she would grieve. She wished to stay there forever.

After the introductions were made, the proprietors led them all upstairs to their rooms. Sadie would be staying in the room called the Tribes, which boasted the castle's original eight-hundred-year-old fireplace with preserved Norman carvings. Emma poked her head inside to take a look, and it was astounding. The very real sense of stepping back in time permeated the entire castle.

As Colin unloaded Sadie's luggage, the rest of them were led to their rooms. Lily, Rose, and Dahlia would be sharing the deBurgo suite. Liam, Daisy, and Emma would occupy the room called the Yeats. Each suite had its own unique personality and décor. Emma would have been happy staying in any of them, and she'd be hard-pressed to choose a favorite.

She helped the three older girls settle into their room, showed them where the bathroom was located, and told them to read a couple of chapters in their books, dangling the promise of some outside time and dinner in their near future. The girls agreed, with only a mild amount of whining. Emma hung their dresses for the wedding in the closet, fluffing each one and imagining how beautiful her daughters were going to look in them. She was thankful that the gowns hadn't wrinkled too much after the long plane ride.

"I'll be back before long. I need to get Daisy cleaned up for dinner, and then we'll take a walk outside and explore the grounds a bit." Emma advised her daughters to be on their best behavior.

Heading down the hall, she heard the happy sounds of Liam and Daisy coming from inside their room. Daisy's giggles made Emma smile, and she knew without even looking that Liam was tickling the toddler. It was Daisy's favorite game to play with Daddy.

"I'm going to go clean myself up a bit. Can you change Daisy's clothes while I do?" Emma asked Liam.

"Of course I can. Your wish is my command, Your Majesty," he replied with a grin and a mock bow.

"Your Majesty?" Emma smirked.

"It seems appropriate, seeing as how we're in a castle and all." Liam laughed good-naturedly.

"Well then, carry on, my humble servant," Emma responded playfully.

While Liam entertained Daisy, Emma ducked into the

bathroom and freshened up from the drive. The group had dinner reservations at one of Liam's and Colin's favorite restaurants, Paddy Burke's Oyster Inn, which was about ten miles from the castle. They'd promised Emma that it would be an experience she would never forget, and she was quite certain they were right. She'd never tried raw oysters, but she'd agreed to give them a go. Emma loved seafood, and she was sure oysters wouldn't be an exception.

She piled her hair into a loose bun and applied some light makeup. Shrugging out of her sweatshirt, she slipped into the emerald-green silk blouse Liam loved before shimmying into her favorite black jeans. It felt good to freshen up, and she was excited about their dinner plans.

As she dug through her suitcase in an attempt to locate her black boots, Emma heard a small clink. It was the distinct sound of something metal dropping onto the age-worn castle floor. Glancing down at her feet, she saw the silver horseshoe necklace Liam had given her on their wedding day, identical to the one she'd given Sadie earlier that morning. Emma picked up the necklace and examined it, crestfallen to discover the clasp had broken.

With a heavy heart, she came to the conclusion that she wouldn't be able to fix it on her own. It saddened her, as it was the first time she'd had it off since Liam placed it around her neck the day they were married. Emma wondered if it was a bad omen. The horseshoe was supposed to bring good luck to a marriage, but that was only a legend. The fact that the necklace had broken was just a coincidence. So why did Emma suddenly have a gnawing, nervous feeling in the pit of her stomach?

Chiding herself for being ridiculous and superstitious, Emma gathered her broken necklace and vowed to have it repaired the minute she returned to Beckland. She assured herself that it was no big deal. Taking one last look at her reflection in the mirror, she decided she was sufficiently put together. She pushed the nagging, foreboding feeling aside and went into the Yeats room, where she placed her broken necklace on the tabletop before letting Liam know she was ready to go to dinner.

A few hours later, after returning from an eventful dinner, Emma tucked her thoroughly exhausted daughters into bed for the night, then attempted to unwind from the whirlwind day. Liam was lying in bed reading, dressed in nothing but his boxers. Daisy slept soundly beside him, completely worn out from their travels.

Emma was tired too, but she was also strangely restless. She still felt a bit jet-lagged, but she'd never been happier. Ireland was an amazing place to visit, with something new to discover at nearly every turn, like fresh oysters at her new favorite restaurant.

Paddy Burke's Oyster Inn had been everything Liam and Colin assured Emma it would be, and the oysters had indeed been delicious. The tangy, slightly slimy, salty mollusks were unlike anything she'd tasted before, but Emma couldn't wait to do it again. Their joyous little group had laughed, reminisced, and spoken with anticipation about the upcoming wedding ceremony. Between the food and company, it had been a perfect night.

With her daughters tucked in and already fast asleep, and Liam in bed as well, Emma decided it was time for her to follow suit. The following day would be an exciting and demanding one. As the matron of honor, Sadie needed Emma to be at her best.

When she grabbed her nightgown from the dresser across the room, Emma noticed her horseshoe necklace wasn't on the table where she'd left it before dinner. Deciding it must have fallen on the floor, she dropped to her hands and knees and scoured the entire area below the table. There was no trace of it anywhere.

She stood to her feet and moved everything around on the tabletop, thinking she must have somehow missed seeing it there. After a thorough search, Emma realized it was nowhere to be found. She glanced around the room, looking for traces of anything else that might be missing. She rifled through her luggage, as well as Liam's, taking stock of their belongings. Everything seemed to be in place, exactly as they'd left it, except for the missing necklace.

Emma had believed the broken necklace was a bad omen, so its disappearance was an even worse one. It seemed that someone had deliberately stolen the necklace but had left all their other belongings alone. It didn't make any sense. While the piece of jewelry had an incomparable amount of senti-mental value, it wasn't particularly expensive. It was just a small silver charm on a plain silver chain, probably not worth more than two hundred dollars. There were far more valuable items in the room that could have been stolen. Why did someone target the broken necklace?

Emma knew she ought to bring it up to Liam, and she almost did. But when she turned to tell him, she saw that he'd already dozed off. She decided she would tell him after the wedding. It was Sadie's big day, and Emma didn't want anything to put a damper on that. She'd let him know what had happened after the ceremony and reception, and then they could try to locate it together.

Discarding her clothing and pulling her nightgown over her head, Emma turned off the light, padded softly across the castle floor, and slipped quietly into bed next to her husband and baby. Although the stolen necklace bothered her greatly, she tried to calm her racing heart and think of the joyous day that awaited them when the sun rose.

TWELVE

THE SOUND OF POUNDING RAIN ON THE CASTLE WINDOWPANE woke Emma from her troubled sleep the following morning. The sense of foreboding she'd felt the night before hadn't drifted away with the darkness as she'd hoped it would. Instead she'd spent the night in fitful slumber, plagued by one nightmare after another.

The dream that was foremost in her memory was of someone chasing her through the Irish countryside. Emma didn't know where she was going, and she had no idea who was after her. All she could recall was terror. The sense of being pursued was all too real, and she shivered under the plush blankets as she remembered.

It had been months since she'd had a nightmare, and there was a moment of panic where she thought that perhaps all her therapy and hard work had been for nothing. It angered Emma that it was happening on her vacation, and she was determined not to let her lack of sleep ruin what was sure to be an otherwise beautiful day.

Sadie needed Emma to be there for her, and that's exactly what she intended to do. It was the matron of honor's role to make sure that the bride's special day went off without a hitch, and that didn't leave any room for feelings of doom and gloom.

Emma scolded herself, quietly slid out of bed, and padded into the bathroom. She hopped into the shower, changed into yoga pants and a T-shirt, and slipped out of the room without waking Liam and Daisy. She ducked her head into the deBurgo suite, where her three older girls were still resting peacefully.

Glancing at her watch, Emma marveled that it was already ten o'clock and all four of her daughters were still asleep. Clearly they had worn themselves out the day before.

Emma knocked quietly on the door of the Tribes room and heard the sound of shuffling feet on the other side. "Good morning, lovely bride." She smiled as Sadie opened the door.

"It's not a good morning—it's the best morning ever." Sadie grinned back. "I'm getting married today!"

Sadie grabbed Emma's hand and pulled her through the door, twirling her around in a joyful dance. Emma pushed aside her own problems and focused on Sadie's happiness. Nothing else mattered at that moment.

"Where's your future husband?" Emma tried to catch her breath as the women stopped dancing.

"I assume he's still in his bedroom, either sleeping or deciding whether or not to run away in fear. We've decided to avoid each other until the ceremony. Colin says it's bad luck for the groom to see the bride on the wedding day." Sadie flopped onto the large bed with a sigh. "The wedding day. Can you believe it, Em? I'm getting married in a few hours!"

"It's been a long time coming, hasn't it? But you and Colin are a perfect match. Your life together is going to be amazing, and I'm so happy for you both." Emma sat on the edge of the bed next to Sadie, trying to forget her broken necklace and the feeling of doom that wouldn't leave her alone.

"It is going to be wonderful, isn't it?" Sadie beamed. "Mom, Eliza, and Fionn should be here soon. They ran to grab us some treats to nibble on while we get ready. They're bringing coffee, too. Are the girls still asleep?"

"Yeah, as hard as that is to believe. I think between jet lag and how busy we've been, they're beat. I'm going to let them sleep as long as possible. We don't want grumpy flower girls, or a petulant ring bearer."

"No we do not. And we both know how cranky those girls can be when they're sleep deprived."

"True. You know my girls just as well as I do. Ever since I had Lily, you've been like a second mom to all of them. I don't know what I would have done without you all of these years," Emma replied quietly, blinking back tears.

"You know I've enjoyed every single second. You and the girls are my family, Em." Sadie's eyes glistened as well.

"After everything that happened with Jacob, and then my parents' death… well… I don't know if I would have survived without you, Sadie. And those aren't just words. I really mean it. You saved my life, you know," Emma whispered as the tears began to fall. Luckily she hadn't yet applied any makeup.

"Oh, Em, I love you so much." Sadie grabbed her friend into a tight hug. "And even though Colin and I are getting married, nothing between us is going to change. You have always been and will always be my soul sister and best friend." Sadie pulled back, still clasping Emma's hands. "I learned a new Gaelic term yesterday: *anam cara*. It means 'soul friend.' That's what we are."

Emma nodded and wiped her face with her T-shirt. As always, Sadie knew the perfect thing to say to make everything better.

"Knock, knock." Eliza's voice greeted the friends as she poked her head through the bedroom door. "Is this a private party, or can we come in?"

"Oh, please come in and rescue us from our blubbering." Emma laughed as she stood from the bed and greeted her mother-in-law with a hug.

"Is everything all right, dear?" Victoria asked her daughter.

"Yes, Mom, everything is fine. Emma and I were just reminiscing about our friendship," Sadie answered.

"What the two of you share goes much deeper than mere friendship. You've been as close as sisters since birth." Victoria placed her bags on the floor and hugged both Emma and Sadie tightly. Victoria had been Emma's mother's best friend, and being close to her always made Emma feel closer to her mother.

"I've been a lucky girl to have you and your daughter in my life," Emma said to Victoria.

"And my son is a lucky man to have you, Sadie, my darlin'," Fionnula interjected.

"Oh, Fionnula, I can't believe he's going to be my husband in just a few hours." Sadie grinned widely at her future mother-in-law.

"I've always wanted a daughter. Thank ya for sharin' yours with me, Victoria." Fionnula gripped Victoria's hand in camaraderie.

"Ladies, we've brought coffee and snacks. Let's have a bite to eat before we start beautifying ourselves." Victoria retrieved the bag containing the food and carried it to the table. She spread the feast on the tabletop, and Emma's stomach growled with hunger. There were blueberry scones, a fruit tray, cheese, crackers, and coffee. It looked delicious, and Emma couldn't wait to dig in.

"Mom, thanks for feeding and caffeinating us. My

stomach is swirling with nerves, but I know I should eat something. I don't want to pass out at the altar," Sadie joked as she grabbed a scone.

"No, you definitely don't want to do that. And don't lock your knees while you're standing there, either," Eliza instructed. "I did that when Duncan and I were married, and I nearly hit the floor."

"I thought my heart would beat out of my chest at my wedding. My palms were so sweaty that when Liam placed the ring on my finger, it nearly slid right off!" Emma poured herself a cup of coffee and added a generous amount of cream and sugar.

"I was steady as a rock, but my Dylan looked absolutely green around the gills at our wedding. I was sure he was gonna lose his breakfast." Fionnula giggled as she fixed herself a plate of food.

"You ladies are making me feel better. Thank you. It's good to know that being nervous is completely normal." Sadie's eyes shone with relief as she nibbled on her scone.

"Darlin', of course it's normal. Bein' nervous just means ya care." Fionnula squeezed Sadie's free hand.

Sadie looked at each woman in the room. "Does anyone have any other advice for me? I'll take all the wisdom I can get today."

"Mostly just remember to enjoy every single second. Today is going to go by so quickly, and when it's over, you'll wish you could go back and do it all over again. Soak it in and appreciate it," Emma responded.

"Hear, hear," the other women replied as they touched their coffee cups together in a toast.

"Is it time to put on our pretty dresses yet, Mama?" Rose asked as she entered the room, followed by Lily and Dahlia.

"Good morning, girls. Why don't you come have some food? It won't be long until we put on our dresses, but you need to eat something first." Emma kissed them each in turn as they filed past her.

"How are my flower girls and ring bearer this morning? Did you sleep well?" Sadie ruffled Rose's hair and hugged Lily and Dahlia.

"We're good. How are you, Aunt Sadie? Are you nervous?" Lily asked.

"Yes, I feel like there are a million butterflies flapping around in my tummy. But I'm very happy, too."

Emma noticed a strange look pass over Sadie's face. Although her words said everything was wonderful, her expression told a different story. Whatever the reason for the look, it was there and gone quickly. No one else noticed it, but Emma had.

As Victoria fixed plates of food for the girls, and Eliza and Fionnula fawned all over them, Emma grabbed Sadie's hand and pulled her aside.

"What's wrong?" Emma spoke quietly, not wanting anyone to overhear their conversation.

"What do you mean?" Sadie chewed her nails and tried to avoid Emma's gaze.

"I know you too well. I saw that look on your face a minute ago. What were you thinking about?"

"I can't really put my finger on it, Em. I'm happier than I've ever been in my life, and I'm definitely not having second thoughts, but there's something... I don't know... off."

"What kind of something?" Emma pushed, needing to know if it was the same feeling she'd been having since the day before.

"It's the sense that something is wrong, the nagging thought that something bad is going to happen. It started yesterday while we were walking around Galway City, and I can't seem to shake it. What do you think it is?" Sadie's eyes widened as she gripped Emma's hands tightly.

Emma wasn't about to tell Sadie that she had the same sense of foreboding. She refused to give voice to whatever that feeling was, lurking just below the surface. It was Sadie's wedding day, and it was Emma's job to keep the focus on that. They shouldn't get caught up in something that probably meant nothing.

Emma squeezed Sadie's hands gently. "It's just normal wedding day jitters. Like I said earlier, sweetie, every bride gets them. You love Colin, and he loves you, and today is going to be magical and perfect. Focus on that. Nothing else is important. You're marrying your Prince Charming in an Irish castle very soon. What can possibly go wrong on such a perfect day?"

Emma hugged her friend and tried to convince herself that what she said was true.

THIRTEEN

DRESSED IN THEIR MATCHING FRILLY IVORY GOWNS, DAHLIA and Rose walked slowly down the aisle to the melodious chords of "The Bride's Return," a traditional Irish wedding song. Daisy, clad in an ivory tutu, grinned from ear to ear as she toddled along holding Dahlia's hand. Emma stood in front of Sadie, encouraging her to breathe as they waited in the wings.

Out of the corner of her eye, Emma watched as her daughters scattered red and pink rose petals down the aisle runner. Lily, who looked quite grown up in her light pink gown, carried Colin's and Sadie's wedding bands on a lacy pillow and followed behind her younger sisters. Emma's heart swelled with maternal pride. Her girls looked just like angels walking down the aisle.

Emma wore a red floor-length chiffon wrap gown that flowed around her body like a scarlet cloud. The sweetheart neckline and crystal gem at the waistline flattered her shape nicely. The look of appreciation on Liam's face when he'd seen her earlier told her all she needed to know.

Sadie held her father's arm nervously, and Emma heard

her friend inhaling and exhaling slowly beside her. The bride might be jittery, but she looked completely stunning in the antique ivory gown that had been worn by generations of women in her family. The wispy, soft chiffon train of the dress flowed effortlessly behind Sadie. The vintage gown had a classic Queen Anne neckline, and Emma spied the small horseshoe necklace resting underneath. The gathered sleeves tucked into beautiful lace wrist cuffs that boasted multiple antique pearl buttons. Sadie's matching veil covered her silky blonde hair like a whisper. Clutching a pink and red rose bouquet, Sadie looked as regal as a queen. Colin's jaw was going to hit the floor when he saw her.

Emma heard the music reach the point where she was supposed to enter. "Are you ready?"

"We're as ready as we'll ever be," Amos answered quietly as he smiled at his daughter.

"I'll see you two at the altar," Emma whispered as she stepped onto the aisle runner.

She walked slowly, smiling her encouragement at Lily, Rose, and Dahlia, who stood silently at the front of the room. Daisy sat happily in the front row, grinning as Duncan bounced her on his knee. Emma's eyes locked with Liam's and her breath caught. She'd never seen him look so dashingly handsome, and she was sure it had something to do with the fact that he was sporting a kilt.

All the O'Reilly men were dressed in their official family tartan, and seeing them all standing there together was nearly more than Emma's heart could take. She'd believed her husband to be gorgeous before, but Liam O'Reilly in a kilt was on an entirely different level. He grinned at his wife, and his dimple made her stomach flip.

The castle was magnificently decorated, and it felt like a royal affair from another era. Candles dripped in the ancient candelabras, and the harpist began playing an ethereal rendition of "Here Comes the Bride" as Emma took her place at the front of the room. The guests stood as Sadie and Amos entered, and Colin's gasp was audible as he took his first look at his bride.

Sadie smiled through her happy tears, and Emma was very glad they'd opted for the waterproof mascara. The minister began the ceremony with a speech about the abundant love they'd witnessed in Sadie and Colin. Emma's heart was filled to the brim with love and happiness for the two of them, and for a few moments, the feeling of foreboding left her.

After Colin and Sadie spoke their heartfelt wedding vows, they exchanged rings. As Colin slipped the wedding band onto Sadie's finger, everyone watched as she turned her beautiful Claddagh ring inward, signifying that she was a married woman. After that, the minister explained that the couple would be quite literally "tying the knot," which was an old tradition symbolizing the bonds of marriage. Sadie and Colin clasped their hands together and the minister wound a red ribbon around their joined hands, cementing their decision to spend their lives together.

The traditions were lovely, and watching her best friend get everything she'd ever wanted brought more tears to Emma's eyes. Once Sadie and Colin were officially declared husband and wife, the minister instructed each guest to ring the small wedding bell that had been placed beneath their seat. It was yet another tradition, originally intended to ward off evil spirits and bring good luck to the marriage. As the sound of ringing bells pealed throughout the room, Colin kissed his bride, and everyone applauded.

The Irish wedding band played "O'Carolan's Concerto" as the wedding party filed happily from the room. There were kisses and hugs and tears of happiness as the guests made their way into the banquet hall. Sadie and Colin were finally husband and wife, and the ceremony had been more beautiful than Emma could have imagined.

She'd been worried for no reason. Everything had gone exactly according to plan. Nothing at all had gone awry. Emma chided herself for letting her wild imagination get the best of her, and then she took her place at the head table with Liam, Sadie, and Colin.

FOURTEEN

The celebratory wedding group may not have been particularly large, but they made up for it in volume. They danced, laughed, and enjoyed the delicious feast Colin had catered for them. The O'Reilly men showed off their innate dancing skills, leading everyone in a traditional step dance. Emma didn't pride herself on being particularly coordinated, but Liam helped her as she muddled her way through the steps. Liam was a wonderful dancer, so Emma just followed his lead.

She enjoyed seeing each and every nuance of her husband's personality. Watching all the men in his family, dressed in kilts, dancing expertly to toe-tapping Irish music, was an eye-opening experience for Emma. To be honest, she'd never really thought of her husband as anything other than an American FBI agent, but since they'd arrived in Ireland, she'd realized that he also had a deep-rooted connection to his heritage. Emma envied Liam's attachment to his family and their history.

When the music stopped, Liam lightly tapped a sparkling

silver utensil on his crystal champagne flute. "Hear, hear. As the best man, I'd like to propose a toast," Liam said above the noise in the room, and everyone took a seat.

"I never thought I'd see the day that my cousin Colin, a self-proclaimed bachelor, would settle down. To be sure, he has found his match in our Sadie. They are two beautiful, wonderful people who I pray will enjoy all of the happiness life has to offer. Colin, if your marriage is even half as wonderful as mine, you'll be doing well." Liam cleared his throat and continued, "I'd like to offer an old Irish blessing to the new couple. 'May God be with you and bless you. May you see your children's children. May you be poor in misfortune, and rich in blessings. May you know nothing but happiness from this day forward. *Slainté!*"

"*Slainté!*" everyone echoed as they clinked their glasses together.

"Thank ya, cousin," Colin said with a smile. "I'm the luckiest man alive to be able to call this lovely woman my wife." He glanced at Sadie, who grinned from ear to ear. "Now I have a special gift for ya, *mo ghrá.*"

Everyone watched expectantly as Colin walked across the room and took his place beside the band. He grabbed the microphone and nodded to the musicians, who clearly knew what was about to happen. The rest of them, including Sadie, had no idea what was coming next.

"This song is dedicated to my beautiful wife, *mo ghrá go deo*, my love forever."

Colin cleared his throat as the music began. He took a deep breath and began to sing "Galway Girl" as the fiddle, guitar, bodhrán, and tin whistle accompanied his velvety voice. The look of surprise on Sadie's face was priceless. She'd obviously been clueless about the fact that her new husband was such a seasoned vocalist.

After he finished the first verse, it was Emma's turn to be surprised.

The band played on, but Colin stopped singing and said, "Liam, come an' join me like in the old days."

Emma glanced at Liam, assuming he would politely decline. Much to her surprise, he sprinted across the room and grabbed the other microphone. As if they'd rehearsed the song for weeks, Liam and Colin blended their voices together in perfect harmony, each man's tone complementing the other.

Emma was stunned. Watching Liam perform was surreal. Her husband was a fantastic singer! She'd had no clue he could sing, not to mention the fact that he could do it so well. Emma's daughters watched in amazement as their father and uncle entertained everyone in the room. It was a moment that none of them would soon forget.

The song ended in deafening applause, and the band went right into a slow tune. Liam walked across the room toward Emma, a mile-wide, dimpled grin on his handsome face.

"I pulled that one out of my sleeve, didn't I?" he asked as he encircled her in his arms. "Did I surprise you?"

"That's the understatement of the year. As a matter of fact, you've been full of surprises this evening, with the kilt, the dancing, and the singing. I feel like I'm getting to know you all over again." Emma grinned widely.

"Well I have to keep you on your toes. I wouldn't want you to get bored with me," he teased, leaning in to kiss her lips passionately.

"No chance of that for at least a hundred years." Emma giggled as their lips parted.

"The girls look like they're having the time of their lives."

Emma glanced across the room to where her daughters were dancing the night away with their grandparents.

"They certainly are. They're going to be full of stories for their friends when we get home." Emma sighed with contentment. She was indeed a lucky woman.

"I can't believe we only have a couple more days here. I'd forgotten how much I love Ireland. Let's make plans to come back soon, all right?" Liam stroked Emma's cheek with his thumb.

"You don't have to ask me twice. I love it here. You know what? I need to go find a restroom. Keep an eye on the girls?" Emma kissed her husband quickly.

"Of course. Hurry back."

Emma wasn't used to wearing heels, and her feet were screaming for mercy. She removed the offending footwear and hurried upstairs to her room to use the bathroom and change into more comfortable shoes. The stone floor was cold beneath her feet, but the sensation was soothing as well. It had been years since she'd spent that much time in heels; she'd be paying the price for it the next day.

Emma reached the top of the staircase and started down the hallway toward her room, her heart and mind filled with happiness at Sadie's perfect wedding day. She hurried, not wanting to miss out on the festivities downstairs.

Reaching for the knob of the bedroom door, she gasped as an icy hand clamped over her mouth. Her scream was muffled, along with her breath. She knew it was a man from the size and shape of his body as he pulled her roughly toward him. She fought against it, but she couldn't move. She tried to scream again, but the sound was stifled.

As he held her in place with one giant palm, he reached around, dangling something shiny in the fingers of his other hand. The faint light from the castle hallway didn't offer much assistance, but Emma made out a glint of silver and a dangling horseshoe. She knew in an instant that it was her missing necklace.

Before she could form another thought, Emma heard a

plinking sound as the necklace hit the stone floor below. With his hand free of the jewelry, he wrapped his fingers around her neck, cutting off her air supply. Emma fought for consciousness, but the effort was pointless. Her body grew limp as she faintly heard the sound of her shoes clattering to the floor.

FIFTEEN

As Emma's body collapsed, Xavier reached down and scooped her into his bulky arms. Burrowing his nose in the fiery silk of her hair, he inhaled the scent of vanilla. Angling his head, he ran his lips across her petal-soft cheek. Too eager to wait, he pressed his lips to hers and reveled in the softness. It would have been more enjoyable if she were awake to return his long-awaited displays of affection, but there would be plenty of time for that.

He kissed her motionless mouth again, then trailed to the hollow of her neck where he allowed his lips to linger for several more seconds. Her skin was just as delicate and velvety as he remembered, and his mind raced wildly with a million thoughts.

He reminded himself to stay focused. As much as he wanted to take the moment slowly, he knew time was not on their side. It wouldn't be long before Emma's presence at the reception was missed, and people would come looking for her. He had to get her out of the castle, and quickly. He hadn't come this far just to lose her again.

With Emma tucked tightly in his arms, Xavier raced

down the hall, away from the grand staircase she had climbed. Obviously he couldn't use the main entrance; that would be foolhardy. He'd leave the same way he entered— through the back door. Unbeknownst to the wedding guests, he'd been at the castle all day, watching the festivities, lurking in the background, and waiting for his golden opportunity.

He'd been there the day before as well. Entering Emma's room while they were at dinner was risky, of course, but he'd needed to feel close to her. He'd needed to smell her perfume and drink in the scent of her. He'd needed to run his fingers over the nightgown she'd left lying across her bed. He'd felt compelled to take her horseshoe necklace. It was an impulsive act, but he'd wanted a trinket of hers to hold him over until he could claim her for his own. He'd dropped the necklace in the process of taking her, but that didn't matter. He had Emma, which was the only thing he really wanted.

Xavier crept down the back stairs. He didn't have long before Emma woke; he had to get her off the castle grounds before her eyes opened and she inevitably started screaming. At that point, his cover would be blown.

Reaching into his pocket, Xavier's fingers found the prefilled syringe, infused with a very strong muscle relaxer. It wouldn't hurt Emma, but it would keep her knocked out much longer. He jabbed the needle beneath her lovely skin and congratulated himself on being prepared.

Wasting no more time, Xavier carried Emma outside under the cover of darkness. He ran across the field and down the road to the small black Volkswagen Golf, the getaway car he'd parked earlier. Ever so gently, Xavier placed Emma in the back seat and jumped behind the wheel.

Starting the car, he sped away from the castle. The boat he'd procured, an Aquastar Ocean Ranger, floated in Galway Bay, waiting for the two of them to sail away into their future. Their final destination would be the remote Shetland Islands, far away from anyone who might know them. It would take them quite a while to get there, but the journey would be as wonderful as the destination.

Xavier had stocked the boat with enough supplies and gas to last them for months, but the first order of business was to get Emma out of Galway before anyone discovered she was gone.

Without a doubt, once Liam realized she was missing, the entire scheme would be traced back to Xavier. None of that mattered, though. He was so close, and nothing was going to stop him.

SIXTEEN

Emma was floating. Her entire body was wrapped tightly inside a thick impenetrable fog, and she was having difficulty moving. She tried to open her eyes, but it was impossible; her eyelids were as heavy as lead. Moaning, she tried to move her legs, but the effort was too great.

The room was moving. Emma's body bobbed up and down in a sort of hypnotic rhythm. Her teeth chattered. She was freezing, though she had no idea why she was so cold. Emma forced her eyes open and glanced around. Nothing looked familiar. She wasn't in the castle, and Liam was nowhere to be seen.

Emma thought she must be dreaming. She reached her hand from beneath the blanket and felt the wall beside her head. The mass was solid and real. It wasn't a figment of her imagination. Clearly she wasn't dreaming.

She took a deep breath and forced her body into a seated position. Her head pounded and her stomach rolled. She closed her eyes tightly and took deep breaths to avoid vomiting, although at that moment, doing so seemed inevitable.

After a few seconds, she tried again to open her eyes.

Once the spinning stopped, she looked around. Emma realized she was on a boat; that would explain the rocking motion. She was inside the cabin. Glancing out the window, she found nothing but inky darkness.

She wondered what time it was. Rubbing her eyes, she tried to stand, but her legs buckled beneath her own body weight. They felt useless, like rubber. She urged herself to think, begged herself to remember, but she had no clue how she'd come to be on a boat, barely able to move.

The last thing she could vividly recall was telling Liam that she had to use the bathroom before heading upstairs to their room. But she'd never made it into the room. Something flashed in her memory, the image of the horseshoe necklace floating to the forefront. Her fingers flew to the hollow of her neck, searching for the jewelry, but she felt nothing. It wasn't there.

Emma remembered seeing the necklace dangling from a strange man's large hand. She recalled the feeling of the man's hand as it gripped her neck and dug in, cutting off her air supply. Those were the only memories she could muster, but they told her enough.

She was in serious trouble.

She gathered her strength and forced herself to stand, begging her useless legs to obey. Leaning on the wall for support, she somehow managed to stay on her feet. Glancing out the small window, she worked hard to get her bearings. There was a dim light in the cabin, and a faint light outside on the deck, but neither offered much assistance.

All she could see for miles around was the black, swirling water of the sea. Panic, fear, and a tangible sense of doom swallowed Emma whole. She knew she had to find a way out.

Glancing around, she noted that the midsized boat was well cared for and comfortable. Stacks of food and clothing lined the cabin walls, and preparations had clearly been made for a lengthy trip. There were enough rations in the room to last for months.

Emma began to hyperventilate. She urged herself to stay calm and to remain rational. There had to be a way out. Things couldn't be as bad as they seemed at that moment.

Try as she might to convince herself, the twisted, knotted feeling in Emma's heart told her that whoever was behind it had obviously concocted an airtight plan. It hadn't been accomplished on a whim. The fact that so much preparation had gone into it, whatever it was, told her she had every reason to be terrified.

"I see you've awakened, Emma."

His voice, like the chilling remnants of a bad dream, cut through the silence of the cabin. Without even turning around, Emma knew who had spoken. It was her worst nightmare come to life. She doubled over as her stomach heaved, releasing its contents onto the floor. Every muscle in her body tightened reflexively, and her legs quivered beneath her, ultimately buckling as she fell into a heap next to the puddle of her own vomit.

Emma didn't move. She couldn't. She prayed fervently that she'd wake and find that none of it was happening, but that wasn't to be. It wasn't a dream. It was real, and she knew exactly what was happening.

Xavier had come back for her, just as he'd always sworn he would.

"Emma, you poor thing. You're overcome with emotion at seeing me again. Let me help you." Xavier knelt beside her and smoothed the hair away from her face.

Emma recoiled but he persisted, grabbing a towel from the table beside them and wiping her mouth.

"Oh no, you've messed up your beautiful hair. Not to worry, we can fix that. Let's get you into the bathroom and clean you up," Xavier said.

Emma protested, but he acted as if he didn't hear her. He was looking at Emma, but his steel-gray eyes peered past her, as if she wasn't even there. She wondered if he saw her at all.

He pulled her to her feet and led her toward the adjoining bathroom, talking the whole time, yet not really saying anything of importance. Emma's body shook involuntarily and she tried to pull away, but his iron grip held her fast.

Xavier led Emma into the bathroom and turned on the shower. She chewed her lip nervously, her intuition screaming about what was coming next. She had to get out of there. She could not allow the thing she feared the most to happen to her.

Her mind raced with ideas for possible means of escape. Every plan led to a dead end. As much as Emma wanted to believe otherwise, she knew there was no getting out of there. They were on a boat in the middle of the ocean; even if she somehow got away from him, there was nowhere to hide.

It was hopeless. She shouldn't even try.

As her brain screamed at her to run, to fight, Emma's body failed to listen. Instead she just stood there, completely compliant. All her determination left her until there was nothing inside but despair. There was no stopping what was about to happen to her, and she knew it.

Xavier unzipped Emma's dress and slowly pulled the red fabric from her shoulders. Tears coursed down her cheeks as she remembered the way Liam had looked at her when he'd first seen her in the dress. She wondered if she'd ever see her husband look at her like that again. Something told her she wouldn't.

Xavier continued pulling the gown away from Emma's body until it dropped into a scarlet heap on the bathroom floor. She shivered in the cold cabin. He turned her body until her back was facing him. Without hesitation, he quickly unhooked each clasp of her bra. Emma gripped the fabric desperately, not wanting to lose the final barrier between them.

She chanted over and over again that it was not happening to her. Told herself that none of it was real. Consoled her fragile mind with the assurance that she would wake up and find herself in her own bed, sleeping beside her husband.

Even as she said the words, she didn't believe them.

Xavier pivoted Emma's body, and she didn't resist. She glanced up at his face. The distant look she'd seen in his eyes only a few minutes before was gone. At that moment, he was aware, and completely invested in what was happening. There was no question in Emma's mind that Xavier knew exactly what he was doing to her.

Lust and greed snapped in his cold eyes, and the look on his face chilled her to the bone. She was completely at his mercy. Emma knew what was coming next, and there was nothing at all she could do to prevent it.

She clutched her bra tightly, but Xavier pried her fingers loose and snatched the garment from her trembling hands. Emma stood before him, completely naked and vulnerable.

"Please," she sobbed, "I'm begging you, don't do this to me. If you have any feelings at all, please take me home."

It was her one last-ditch effort to appeal to any trace of his humanity.

Xavier's locked eyes with her. "Home? My darling, Emma, you are home. Now let's clean you up. Your hair reeks of vomit."

He grabbed her arm and led her to the shower. Placing his hand under the stream, he checked the temperature before he forced her inside. Emma's brain yelled for her to fight back, but she didn't. There was no fire left. She'd escaped Xavier once already, and then she'd escaped Morgan. Both times she'd fought as hard as she could to get away.

This time, everything felt different. Nothing mattered. Xavier had won. Nothing she did would ever make him stop. She'd never be free of him.

Emma had lived in fear of him for years. She'd had nightmares about him coming back for her. He had such a grip on her mind that she'd needed therapy to regain any semblance of a normal life. In the end, none of it mattered. Her worst dreams had come true. Fighting Xavier Smith was pointless. She'd been lucky before, but her luck had run out. There would be no escaping.

As the black hole of numbness overtook her, she became like a puppet, with Xavier the puppet master pulling all the strings. She told herself not to feel it, commanded her mind to go somewhere else. She repeated the instructions over and over again.

The hot water cascaded over her as she stood motionless in the shower. Emma escaped the shell of her body, feeling as if she were perched in the corner of the room watching everything happen to her. It was easier that way, like the trauma was happening to someone else.

Xavier squirted vanilla-scented body wash onto a cloth and lathered it, then ran it over her body with gentle hypnotic motions as he washed every inch of her skin. She didn't allow herself to flinch as his hands touched her skin when he moved her body under the water and rinsed the soap away. He covered her wet hair with fruity-smelling shampoo and massaged it into her scalp, not missing a single spot.

As he rubbed Emma's head, she was sickened to realize that it actually felt good, the thought making her want to vomit again. The man was a psychopath. It seemed impossible that anything he did could feel good. Something was terribly, irrevocably wrong with her.

She began to talk to herself once again, telling herself it

was pretend, that she was watching a movie in a theater. She soothed herself, reassuring her vulnerable mind that nothing could touch her. Still, guilt and shame washed over her like the cascading water, and she understood that Xavier had broken her. She'd lost touch with reality. Xavier had finally driven her over the edge.

The only way Emma could cope with the madness was to think of Liam. She pretended she was with her husband. She imagined Xavier's hands were Liam's. Like a woman drowning, Emma clung for dear life to her delusions. She closed her eyes and allowed Xavier to do what he was going to do, consoling herself with the ruse that it was her husband who was doing it.

As she felt Xavier's lips on her neck, and as his hands slid over her body, Emma thought of Liam. When Xavier roughly claimed her mouth with his own, it was her husband's face she saw. It was the only way Emma could handle what she knew was coming next.

SEVENTEEN

INSTEAD OF GREETING THE NEW DAY QUIETLY, THE OCCUPANTS of Cloghan Castle had been awake all through the night. When Liam discovered Emma was missing, the wedding festivities came to a halt and the investigation began. Pandemonium broke loose in the normally peaceful venue. Wedding guests had transformed into search parties, and the authorities had been called in.

Every inch of the castle was scoured, but Emma was nowhere to be found. The castle grounds had all been inspected, but there was no sign of her. The only piece of evidence was Emma's broken horseshoe necklace, which had been found on the floor outside of her bedroom. When he saw it, Liam knew without a doubt that his wife was in grave danger. Seeing the lucky trinket he'd given her on their wedding day lying broken on the castle floor was enough to let him know that their good fortune had run out.

Lily, Rose, Dahlia, and Daisy had cried all night long, begging someone to bring their Mama home. The girls were inconsolable. Fionnula, Eliza, and Victoria did their best to comfort them, but there was little they could do. Meanwhile,

Sadie, Colin, and Liam worked to come up with strategies to find Emma.

"I knew something was wrong, Liam. I knew it! I told Emma yesterday. I had a sense that something horrible was going to happen, and she told me it was just wedding jitters. Why didn't I listen to my feelings?" Sadie, who had been pacing back and forth across the castle floor, slumped desperately into a nearby chair.

Colin gathered his new wife into his arms and stroked her back soothingly. "You canna be blamin' yourself, *mo ghrá*. None o' this is your fault, and I'll not be havin' ya take it on as if it were."

"Colin's right, Sadie. Blaming yourself isn't going to help us find her." Frustrated, Liam ran his hands through his hair. "What are we missing? There's something we aren't seeing here. Emma didn't just wander off. She's gone because someone took her."

"I hate to say it, Liam, but I know we're all thinking the same thing. This isn't the first time Emma's been taken. Xavier was behind it before, and I'm willing to bet my life that somehow he's behind it again," Sadie said quietly.

"I know it. I've been telling myself not to go there, but I know it's the truth. How did he get to her in Ireland? The Ohio State Pen informed me three months ago that Xavier was part of the prison break, but they assured me that everything had been taken care of. Now I know I wasn't told the whole story. I need to call them." Liam grabbed his phone and punched in the number.

Liam spoke succinctly to the person on the other end of the phone. Colin and Sadie watched as the look of irritation on his face turned to shock, then anger. Sadie gripped her husband's hand tightly as they waited.

"What did you just say to me?" Liam's thunderous voice tore through the silence of the room. "Why wasn't I informed of this?" He spewed a string of profanities at the person on the other end before hanging up and angrily stuffing the phone into his pocket.

"What is it, Liam?" Colin asked, even though he likely already knew the answer.

"Xavier is gone. Apparently he has been for quite some time. It wasn't important enough to inform me that the monster who tried to kill my wife is a free man." Liam swore again and pounded his fist on the wooden table in front of him.

"What do you mean he's out?" Sadie asked tearfully.

"Do you remember the news covering that prison break right around Thanksgiving? Well, we knew Xavier was a part of it, but I was assured it had all been taken care of. Obviously the corruption runs far deeper than I thought. They've known all along that he was gone, but decided not to inform me about it so they could sweep the fiasco under the rug. Now I'm sure Xavier's behind this. I know it!"

Liam began to pace back and forth across the floor.

"A'right, Liam. Let's think." Colin rose and put his hand on his cousin's shoulder. "Xavier found out we're in Ireland, and he figured he'd take her from here. He's not gonna stay in Ireland any longer than he has to. He's gonna get her as far away from here as he can. So, how's he gonna do it? He's not gonna fly her out. That's too risky."

"You're right. He's going to try to escape either by land or by sea. We have to search both."

"I'll call in every person I know to help. We will find her, Liam," Colin assured.

"We have to," Liam said quietly.

EIGHTEEN

Emma lay as still as she could in the large bed, hoping Xavier would leave her alone if he thought she was asleep. She was drained, and she had no idea how she could survive another second with the madman. The acts she'd been subjected to over the last five days made her want to weep, but she couldn't even manage to do that. It was as if all her tears had run dry and she had no emotions left inside.

Her body had been violated, and the only thing that kept her going was picturing her husband's face in her mind as she was forced to obey the commands. Each night, Emma dreamed of her daughters. Their small voices cried out to her in the darkness, and she searched frantically, but they were nowhere to be found. Every time she slept, she dreamed of them. The terror was too much, and Emma was afraid to close her eyes for fear of hearing them call to her again. Instead, she fought to stay awake. The horror of reality was better than the desperation of knowing she couldn't reach her children.

Xavier moved in the bed beside her, and her stomach clenched. She knew what would happen once he was awake.

She tried to lie as still as she could, but she flinched when his arms wrapped around her. He pulled her toward him.

"Good morning, my beautiful Emma," he whispered in her ear. "Did you sleep well?"

"Yes, I did. I slept very well," she lied.

She'd figured out quickly that it was better to just go along with his ruse.

"I'm looking forward to spending another day with you. All of that time apart just made me realize how much I love you. Our life together is going to be so wonderful. Although I haven't been sensing as much enthusiasm in you as I'd hoped." Xavier began caressing Emma's back.

"I'm sorry," she replied quietly.

"I'm not heartless, Emma. I understand that you've been brainwashed into believing you love Liam O'Reilly. I'm willing to give you some time to realize your true feelings for me. Once you do, darling, we're going to be so happy together. I've gone through so much to be with you."

Xavier turned Emma's face toward his and kissed her. She tried her best to respond appropriately, so as not to anger him. She pictured Liam's face in her mind as she did. Xavier pulled away and looked at her, and she could tell he'd been temporarily appeased. The more she could keep him talking, the longer she could delay the inevitable.

"I'm trying, Xavier. I really am. But I do miss my children. You must understand that," Emma explained.

"Of course I understand. You're a mother, after all. But your children have a lot of people to look after them. They will be well taken care of. I know you're the nurturing type— it's one of the many reasons I love you so much—so I've decided we will have children of our own. A whole houseful of them, if that's what you want." Xavier smiled widely, as if he'd just offered her a million dollars.

Emma's heart beat frantically as she thought of the horror of producing a child with the monster.

"Children? You plan for us to have children?" Emma questioned him desperately, praying she'd heard him wrong.

"Of course. That's what couples do, isn't it? Procreate?" Xavier laughed at her obvious surprise.

"I... I can't... have... more children," she lied. "I had complications when I had Daisy, and I was told I couldn't have any more."

Emma needed him to stop talking about having children with her. The mere thought of the possibility was too much for her desperate mind to grasp.

"Hmm... I didn't expect that. I had intended to give you children. I suppose we don't have to decide everything today, of course. We have our whole lives to figure it all out." He smiled and stroked her hair.

"Where are we going, Xavier? We can't stay on this boat forever." Emma spoke softly, hoping her questions wouldn't provoke him.

"Have you ever heard of the Shetland Islands? It's a lovely little island chain to the northeast of Scotland. It's the perfect place for us to make our home. It's quiet and remote, so we won't be disturbed. No one will know us there, and we can make a fresh start," Xavier answered with a grin as he again covered her mouth with his.

Emma knew no one would ever find her in the Shetland Islands. Any hope she had of being rescued was gone.

With Xavier's words, Emma's fate was sealed. She would never see her husband and daughters again.

NINETEEN

Two days later, Colin and Liam scoured the streets of Galway City. They had conducted a ground search over the past few days, but nothing had turned up. After much thought, Colin and Liam came to the conclusion that Xavier had taken Emma away by boat. They'd plastered "Missing" posters with Emma's picture on every surface in town and prayed for the tips to come rolling in. So far, they had received a few, but in the end none of them had panned out.

"We need to hit the marina next. We'll talk to every person there and anyone who has ever owned a boat in the town. She's already been gone a week. We're running out of time," Liam said.

"Indeed we are. Let's go," Colin agreed.

The two men spoke with every person they met by the water. They went up and down the marina, interviewing all of the boat owners. They asked if any strangers had been poking around asking questions. The locals were cooperative, but no one could recall seeing anyone suspicious. Finally they came to the end of the marina, where they spotted a man washing a shiny, obviously new boat.

"Excuse us, sir. Can we ask you a few questions?" Liam said to the man, who stopped washing his boat when he saw them approach.

"Sure can. What can I do for you?" he replied in a thick Irish accent.

"Over the past couple of weeks, have you seen a man around the marina asking questions about buying or renting a boat? The man would have been tall, muscular, with an American accent?" Liam prodded.

"I think I might have. A couple of weeks ago, this big burly man flashed a pile of cash at me. He asked if I was interested in selling my Aquastar Ocean Ranger. She was a decent boat, but she wasn't worth the sum of money the man offered me. I'd have been crazy to say no. I told him sure, I'd sell her to him for that price. That's how I bought my new boat." The man smiled broadly and gestured toward the vessel.

"And this man, he paid cash?" Colin questioned.

"Sure did. Handed me the biggest pile of American money I've ever seen in my life. He even wrote me out a receipt for it. I cleared my stuff from the boat, and he told me he'd have it moved within the week. He sailed it out of the bay several nights ago. I just bought this beauty yesterday."

"You said he wrote you a receipt for the boat. Would you mind if I took a look at it?" Liam asked.

"Sure, you can see it if you want. But it's a done deal. I didn't do anything wrong," the man said warily.

"No, of course not, sir. We're simply following up on a lead. May I see the receipt?" Liam prompted.

The man fished around in his pockets and pulled out a wrinkled piece of paper. Liam skimmed over the outra- geous price that had been paid for the boat and went straight to the signature at the bottom. He blinked and read the name again. Xavier Smith wasn't anywhere to be found on the handwritten receipt. But the name Jacob McCoy was.

Liam's heart sank in his chest as he handed the scrap of paper to Colin, who also examined it. The men's eyes locked on one another as they realized what was happening.

"Sir, did the man who bought your boat happen to mention where he was headed?" Liam asked quickly.

"He sure did. He said he'd always wanted to see the Shetland Islands. I told him he was crazy to want to go somewhere so remote, but he said it was just what he was looking for." The man chuckled. "Can I have my receipt back?"

"I'm sorry, sir, but I'm going to need to hang on to it."

"Well okay. I guess I don't need it."

"Thank you for your time," Liam said, and he and Colin walked briskly away from the water, stopping once they were out of earshot of the man.

"You know what this means? Jacob McCoy? Xavier has assumed the identity of Emma's dead husband. That's how he's managed not to get caught."

Liam's brain was running laps inside of his head, and he tried to corral his thoughts. He needed to think clearly if he was going to find a way out of this.

"Excuse me, please."

Liam turned around as he heard the sound of someone approaching them from behind. It was the man from the marina.

"Yes? I'm sorry, sir, but we really need to keep this receipt. We can make a copy of it for you, but we need it for the investigation," Liam said quickly, not wanting his thoughts to be disturbed by the man.

"It's not about the receipt. I don't care about that. I've already spent the money anyway. It's just that I thought of something else that might be helpful," the man replied.

"What's that, sir?" Colin asked.

"Well, you see, the Aquastar I sold him has a GPS locator on it. I had it installed a few years ago in case I ever got lost out at sea."

"You mean the boat can be tracked?"

"Sure it can. It might take a bit, but we can triangulate its general location. Will that help?" he asked hopefully.

"Yes, it will. Thank you, sir." Liam shook the man's hand as the first glimmer of hope sprang into his heart.

TWENTY

Another night of unspeakable acts faded into one more day as Xavier's hostage. Emma had lost count of how long she'd been gone. All she knew was that an endless, hopeless expanse of time lay before her. One day bled into the next, and she grew more and more despondent.

She was sleep deprived, her body was weary, and there was no hope of being rescued. As the sun peeked through the cabin window, she cursed it and begged it to go away. Emma didn't want to face the future.

She watched as Xavier prepared breakfast for them. He waited on her hand and foot, and other than the obvious fact that he was holding her prisoner, he wasn't cruel. Although he'd made her do countless things she hadn't wanted to, he wasn't rough about it. Of course, she'd been compliant; if she'd fought back, it might have been a different story.

His touch repulsed her, and she'd considered resisting his advances a few times, but she was too afraid to actually follow through. So she'd gone along with every bit of it, all the while telling herself it was Liam. It was the only reason she still had even a tiny grip on her sanity, although every day it slipped further away.

"It looks like the sun is peeking out from behind the clouds this morning. I think we should eat our breakfast topside. You're looking pale. You should soak up some Vitamin D, my love," Xavier said as he plated the food.

"If that's what you want. I'll get dressed," Emma replied obediently.

"There's no need to waste your time with that. I like you just the way you are." He chuckled. Xavier didn't allow Emma to sleep in anything besides a nightshirt. "Just pull the blanket around you in case you get cold."

"All right," she responded robotically.

Emma wrapped the blanket tightly around her scantily clad body and followed Xavier up the stairs to the deck, where she took a seat at the table. She didn't have much of an appetite, but she pushed the food around anyway. Xavier grew angry if she didn't eat, so she had to at least look like she was.

"It's certainly a beautiful morning, isn't it, my dear?" Xavier said jovially.

"Yes it is," she replied listlessly, finally raising her head to take a look around.

The sun shone brightly, and its rays warmed her. The ocean glistened like diamonds, surrounding the boat on all sides. Regardless of the circumstances, Emma had to admit that it truly was a lovely morning. It reminded her of the last day she'd spent with Liam and the girls before Sadie's wedding. It had been a perfect day when anything seemed possible. She'd taken days like that for granted, believing she'd always have the luxury of spending time with her family.

Since Emma had been on the boat, she'd pushed aside all thoughts of her family. It was torture to think of them, so her brain had existed in a fog. She didn't allow herself to dwell too long on anything. She simply obeyed Xavier's commands in hopes of staying alive. She didn't let her mind wander any more than that. She'd forced herself to become numb, trying her best not to feel anything.

But as Emma sat there that morning, pushing the food around on her plate, she gave herself permission to remember. A series of perfect little moments began to play in her mind. She recalled the day that she'd given birth to each of her daughters. She remembered the feeling of pure, complete love when she'd looked at each of their faces. She thought of how she'd promised she would always be there for them.

She recalled the day she'd met Liam, and how it had felt like being struck by lightning. She replayed their wedding day in her mind, and held on to the feeling of finally coming home. She remembered the vows they'd made to spend the rest of their lives together.

With a jolt, Emma realized she was far from finished with her life.

As each little moment resurfaced, something began to happen inside of her. The fog in her brain began to clear, and Emma saw everything with crystal vision. The fear began to leave, and boldness started to take shape. The lifelessness in her body was replaced by anger and adrenaline. The despair dissipated, and she felt tiny ripples of hope. She didn't know where it was coming from, but as she thought about Liam and her daughters, the feelings continued to grow.

Sadie had always joked that Emma was Superwoman, and suddenly she felt like she was. At that moment, she believed herself capable of anything. When faced with a life-or-death situation, a person's fight or flight reflex kicked in. Since the day Xavier kidnapped Emma, she'd been on the retreating end, but that was finished. The time had come for her to fight.

Liam couldn't rescue her. No one was coming to save her. If she had any hope of continuing her life, it was up to her to make it happen. In that instant, she decided she wasn't going down without a fight. She refused to comply for another second. Either Emma or Xavier wouldn't get out of it alive, and she understood it would more than likely be her. The odds were highly stacked against her, but she was determined to see her family again or die trying. The time for being numb was over.

Emma watched as Xavier shoveled food into his mouth while he talked about all the things they were going to do once they reached the Shetland Islands. She determined that once and for all, she was taking control of the situation. She would not allow that psychopath to rob her of her husband and children. He wasn't stealing her future, and if he tried to, she would not go willingly.

She glanced around the boat for a weapon and noticed a gaff hook hanging on the wall behind Xavier. Unfortunately, she couldn't get to it without going past him. Next to the gaff hook was a thick rope that was anchored to the floor of the deck. The other end of the rope was thrown over the edge of the boat. Emma scanned her surroundings, but other than the silverware, there was nothing within reach that she could use.

Determined not to give up, she pretended to eat breakfast as her brain ran a thousand miles an hour. Out of the corner of her eye, she spotted a large bottle of some type of cleaning solution. She adjusted the chair, scooting it a bit closer to the container. Emma could barely read it, but she was fairly certain she saw the words *muriatic acid* across the front.

She knew the liquid was used for cleaning and descaling. She wasn't an expert on chemicals, but she knew enough to understand it was harmful. Muriatic acid was corrosive, and its noxious odor could be dangerous. It was her best hope.

Somehow, she had to get Xavier below deck so she could get her hands on the bottle.

"Xavier, I hate to be a bother, but could I have some more coffee, please? It's delicious," Emma lied as she guzzled the remainder of the black liquid inside of her mug.

"Of course. I'm happy to see that you're at least enjoying the coffee. You've hardly touched your food," he replied with a scowl.

"I'm trying. It's just that I'm not used to being on a boat. I'm sure once we reach land, my appetite will come back," she answered quickly.

"Very well. I'll go get you more coffee," he said with a smile as he grabbed her mug and disappeared below deck.

Emma's heart raced, but she told herself to ignore it. It might be her only chance at escape, and she needed to keep a level head. She jumped out of the seat, grabbed the bottle of muriatic acid, unscrewed the cap, and gripped it tightly in her trembling hands. She waited quietly as she watched the stairs, not allowing herself to even blink. She heard heavy footsteps, then spied the top of Xavier's head as he rounded the corner.

Without a moment's hesitation, Emma lunged toward him, throwing the acidic liquid in his face. He let out an agonizing scream as the noxious odor wafted through the air. Emma coughed and sputtered, covering her mouth with the blanket as she backed away from him. Xavier's hands flew to his eyes and he began to rub them, cursing her all the while. He tore at the skin on his face as he moaned in agony. The more he rubbed, the more the acid damaged his skin.

Emma heard it sizzle on his flesh, but she told herself not to think about it. She was doing what she must to stay alive. The cleaning solution was highly concentrated, so the damage would be severe and irreparable. She was counting on it.

As he continued to scream, Emma tossed the remainder of the liquid at him. Much to her surprise, instead of incapacitating him, the pain seemed to energize him. He lunged at her, blindly flailing his giant fists and making contact with her face. Emma's head snapped back from the force, and she grabbed the table for support.

She backed farther away from him, but he pursued her. Xavier could barely see, but that didn't slow him down. He was propelled by sheer anger and insanity, and although she'd momentarily sidetracked him, Emma was still very much in danger.

She turned and darted across the floor, but he reached out and blindly grabbed at her blanket, causing her to trip in the process. Her body plummeted to the ground and she slid across the deck, crashing into the boat's wall.

"You're going to pay, Emma!" Xavier screamed as he pursued her.

"You'll have to kill me if you want me to stay here. I will not willingly spend another second on this boat with you," she yelled back.

He reached down and grabbed her by the hair, yanking her to a standing position. He was leaning against the edge of the boat, and Emma took a deep breath and slammed her body into his, hoping to stun him. Instead, the force of her body crashing into his caused him to lose his balance. He teetered and tried to catch himself, but he careened over the edge.

As his feet left the deck's surface, he grabbed Emma's arm and pulled her overboard with him. He held tightly to her as they hit the surface of the water, where they were quickly swallowed up by the frigid waves. Emma kicked her legs, elbowed him, and tried to wriggle free of his grasp. Surprisingly, he released his grip and she swam upward.

As her head popped out of the water, she took a deep

breath, sputtering and coughing as her lungs screamed for air. It was February, and the water was freezing. Emma knew staying in it too long meant her death sentence, but her body was so cold that it moved in slow motion. She willed her legs to kick harder and her arms to propel her faster, but she progressed slowly toward the boat.

Emma looked behind her to determine Xavier's whereabouts, and she saw his body bobbing about in the water a few feet away. He wasn't moving, and she wondered if he'd passed out. She prayed he was dead.

She continued struggling through the water and eventually reached the vessel. She had no idea how to get herself back on board, but she had to get out of the freezing ocean before hypothermia set in. Gripping the boat's side, she pulled herself around to the stern, where she'd seen the hanging rope. She hoped it was still there, and she nearly cried with relief when she saw that it was.

Emma mustered all the strength she had and hoisted her body upward as she planted her freezing, bare feet on the boat's side for support. She shivered violently, having nothing to cover her body except a soaking-wet, paper-thin nightshirt. Her legs nearly buckled beneath her, but she urged her body onward.

She'd managed to pull herself almost to the top before her feet slipped and she plunged back into the icy depths below. Once more, she swam toward the water's surface, gripped the rope firmly in both hands, and pulled herself up. She was determined to see her husband and children again, no matter what it took.

Finally she made it to the top, throwing her arm over the side of the boat to ensure she wouldn't fall again. She tried flinging the rest of her weary body on board, but she didn't have the strength; she hung there, the top half of her body

draped over the edge and the bottom half dangling precari-
ously above the water.

Emma was exhausted. She wanted to go to sleep. She'd
have given anything at that moment to drift off into peaceful
slumber, but she knew she had to stay awake. She ran her
hand over the inside edge of the boat and felt a wooden stick
beneath her fingertips. Her heart beat faster when she realized it was the gaff hook she'd spotted hanging on the wall
behind Xavier during breakfast. She held on tightly to the
side of the boat with one hand and pulled the gaff hook out
of its wall mount with the other. She had no idea how to use
it, but having it at her disposal seemed like a good idea.

Glancing around, she looked for Xavier. She had to keep
him in her sights. She needed to know where he was at all
times. Her eyes darted across the surface of the water, but
she didn't see him anywhere. She thought he might be dead.
Perhaps he'd died from inhaling the acid fumes. Maybe he'd
drowned.

Emma continued looking around, but her captor was
nowhere to be seen. She worked to come up with a plan to
get herself back on the deck of the boat. Her arms wouldn't
support her hanging body forever, and she couldn't bear to
think of plunging into the freezing water again.

She gingerly placed the gaff hook on the side of the boat.
With one hand, she wrapped the thick rope around her wrist
several times, in essence tethering herself to the side of the
vessel. With her free hand, she grabbed the gaff hook once
again. She tried to push herself over the edge by walking her
bare feet along the outside of the boat, but every time she
tried, they slipped.

Suddenly something tugged on her ankle. She looked
over her shoulder and saw Xavier's arm reaching out of the
water.

Emma kicked her legs wildly and tried to get away from

him, but doing so caused her grip to slip on the edge of the boat. She nearly lost her hold, but luckily she was still securely tethered by the rope. Grabbing the gaff hook pole tightly in the hand that wasn't tied to the boat, she swung it at Xavier with all her might. She missed.

"Emma, I love you. Why are you doing this to me? To us?" Xavier called out desperately.

She took a deep breath, her stomach lurching because she knew exactly what she needed to do to survive. She pictured her husband and daughters, held the image firmly in her mind as she imagined herself home with them.

She took a deep breath, screamed loudly, and aimed the sharp end of the hook at Xavier's face. Gagging as the pointed end made contact with his flesh, she dug the gaff hook directly into his eye as he unleashed a blood-curdling scream that she would never forget.

Once the hook was in his eye socket, Emma tugged the stick end toward her, sinking the weapon firmly into place. Blood and liquid spewed from his face and his body immediately went limp. She wondered if she'd killed him. She didn't know if a person could live through having his eye gaffed.

Emma watched as Xavier's motionless body, skewered on the end of the gaff hook, floated in the blood-tinged water below.

She'd finally won. She'd killed him. He was gone.

Her vision grew blurry and everything around her went dark.

TWENTY-ONE

Liam intently scanned his surroundings as the Coastguard Agency lifeboat he was riding on sped through the water. The search and rescue helicopter circled in the blue sky above. Thanks to the tip from the man who had sold the boat to Xavier, they'd been able to successfully triangulate the boat's coordinates.

Xavier's boat was sailing in the waters north of Scotland, and Liam knew they were getting close. He had no idea what they might find once they arrived, but he'd worked hard to prepare himself for the worst. It was the third time Emma had been targeted, and he was rational enough to realize their luck was running out.

He hadn't slept in days, and his sanity was dangling by a thread, but he had to find his wife. He'd sworn to his daughters that he would bring their mama home, and if it was humanly possible, he intended to keep that promise.

"We see it up ahead."

Liam heard the search and rescue worker's voice through the speaker on the boat and his heart nearly stopped. He made his way to the front of the lifeboat to get a better look.

The Aquastar Ocean Ranger Xavier had purchased from the man at the marina bobbed up and down in the water. Liam didn't see any movement on the deck, and he wondered if they were in the cabin below. He prayed he would find his wife safe and sound.

"Xavier Smith, come out onto the deck with your hands up. We are boarding your vessel," the coxswain of the lifeboat commanded through the speaker.

They waited several seconds, and when they received no response, the water bailiff who was in charge boarded the Aquastar. He searched the boat thoroughly, but Liam could tell he didn't find anyone. Suddenly the water bailiff spotted something and signaled for the other men to board the boat.

Liam had tried to remain patient, but he could wait no more. He quickly jumped on board the Aquastar and ran to the edge of the vessel where the water bailiff stood. His heart nearly stopped dead in his chest when he saw his precious Emma hanging over the edge, secured in place by nothing but the rope that was twisted around her wrist. She was unconscious, and her pale skin had taken on a blue-gray tint.

Liam pushed the other men aside and grabbed the rope, tugging as hard as he could and pulling Emma's limp body over the side of the boat. He cradled her in his arms while he unwound the rope from her wrist, cursing to himself as he saw the damage that had been done.

Placing her still form on the deck of the boat, he felt for a pulse but couldn't find one. He laid his head on her chest, praying he would detect a breath, but he couldn't.

"Help her. Please, someone, help my wife," Liam screamed as he gathered her body to his and sobbed.

He rocked her back and forth, trying to force his own strength into her, but it was no use. About that time, the paramedic from the rescue helicopter came on board and gently pried Emma's body from Liam's arms.

"Sir, please let me try to help her," he coaxed when Liam refused to let her go.

"She can't be dead. It's not possible. You have to do something," Liam cried as he placed Emma on the deck of the boat.

"I am going to do everything within my power to help your wife."

Moving quickly, the emergency worker tried to find a pulse, but his frown didn't offer much reassurance. Finally his face lit up and he turned to Liam.

"Her pulse is very slow, and her breathing is shallow, but she's alive. We're taking her on the helicopter and transporting her to the nearest hospital. You can come with us."

"Thank you," Liam managed in between his sobs.

Emma, Liam, and the paramedic were hoisted one at a time from the boat into the helicopter. Once they were on board the chopper, Liam grabbed Emma's hand and held on tightly, begging her to stay with him.

Although they had found her, she was barely alive, and there was no guarantee she would make it.

TWENTY-TWO

EMMA WOKE UP IN A HOSPITAL ROOM SOMEWHERE IN Scotland. She knew where she was based on the accents of the doctors and nurses buzzing around in the room. When her eyelids fluttered open, the first thing she saw was Liam sitting beside her bed with a mile-wide, dimpled grin on his handsome, weary, worried face. Tears glistened in his eyes as he leaned in and kissed her tenderly on the forehead.

"Hey there, sleepyhead. I was wondering when you were going to open those beautiful eyes of yours," he said quietly as he gripped her hand tightly.

"Liam…." She tried to speak but it was difficult. Her mouth felt like cotton, and she knew she must be dehydrated.

"I need water." Her voice cracked, forcing her to whisper hoarsely.

Liam grabbed a cup from the bedside table, filled it with water and a straw, and brought it to her mouth. She sipped the liquid greedily, thinking she would never have her fill.

"Go slowly. You don't want to get nauseated," Liam warned.

She nodded. "Where are the girls?" She wanted to hold her children more than she'd ever wanted anything.

"Sadie and Colin will be here with them soon," her husband assured her.

"How long have I been here?" Emma had no idea how long she'd been asleep.

"We found you five days ago. You've been in and out of consciousness ever since. You gave me a pretty good scare."

"I gave myself a pretty good scare. To be honest, I have no idea how I'm still alive. I thought for sure I was dead." Her voice broke with emotion.

"You're not the only one. Can you remember anything that happened?"

"I remember everything that happened. I'll never be able to forget it."

Slowly, Emma began to relay the sordid story to her husband.

"You threw acid in his face and gaffed him in the eye?" The shock in Liam's voice was obvious.

"I did," she replied with a shudder. "I knew I had to kill him if I was going to get away. I had to finish him off once and for all so he could never come after me again."

"Emma, you are the bravest person I've ever known," Liam said as his voice cracked.

"Where did you take his body? I need to see it."

"His body? Emma, his body wasn't recovered," Liam answered slowly.

"What do you mean? I watched him bleed to death. I stuck the gaff hook into his eye and I held onto it. I didn't let go. Are you telling me he wasn't there when you found me?" She couldn't believe what she was hearing.

"Emma, when we found you, you were unconscious. The only reason you didn't drown was because your wrist was tethered to the boat. If you hadn't thought to tie yourself with the rope, you would have been washed away just like he was." Liam shivered at the thought.

"You think his body was washed away?" She refused to believe he wasn't dead.

"The Coast Guard has been searching, but his body hasn't been recovered."

"He's dead. I know he is, Liam. He has to be. He was bleeding so much." She threw up her hands in desperation. "I can't ever lead a normal life if he's not dead."

"If a gaff hook to the eye didn't kill him, then hypothermia did. You had nearly frozen to death when we found you, and you weren't even in the water. There is no way Xavier Smith survived. Whether or not his body is ever found, I'm telling you that you killed him, Emma. The nightmare is over."

Liam pulled her trembling body close to his and whispered over and over that Xavier was gone until she finally believed it.

A couple of hours later, the entire family arrived. Emma sobbed when she saw her daughters, grabbing tightly to them and holding on. She swore she'd never leave them again, vowing to herself that she would cherish every single moment with them, even the crazy, tiresome ones. She would never let herself forget that she almost lost everything.

When Sadie saw Emma, she gripped her so tightly that she could hardly breathe.

"I thought we'd lost you, Emma. I don't know what I would have done," Sadie whispered through her tears.

"I know. I thought so, too. For a while, I lost all hope. I just knew I wasn't going to get out alive. But then I decided I would fight back, no matter what. I wasn't going to stop until I saw you all again. I kept hearing you call me Superwoman, Sadie, and somehow that's what I became."

"You've always been a superhero in my eyes, Em."

"I realized I couldn't check out just yet. You're going to need my advice on surviving marriage to an O'Reilly man. It can certainly be an adventure." Emma laughed.

"That's the truth of it. We're also gonna need your parenting advice real soon, love." Colin smiled as he kissed Emma on the cheek.

"Parenting advice? Does that mean...?"

She glanced back and forth from Colin to Sadie, and the joy that shone from their faces told her all she needed to know.

"I've suspected it for a while, but I just found out for certain. I would have told you, but I didn't want to jinx it by talking about it too soon. If I'm even half as good a mom as you are, Em, I'll consider myself a success." Sadie grinned through her tears.

"You're going to be the best mom ever. There's not a doubt in my mind." Emma squeezed her best friend's hand tightly.

She looked around the hospital room at the faces of those she loved more than life itself. She closed her eyes, whispered a prayer of thanks, and pictured her parents smiling down on her. Emma had been to Hell and back more than once over the past several years, but she'd survived.

Without a doubt, she knew it was because of the love of the people who were crowded into that tiny room. Knowing they needed her had given her the strength and determination to make it through everything life had thrown her way. She'd found her hope and her reason in them. When her own will to survive had left her, she'd fought back for the people she cared for the most. Their love was what had saved her.

"I have something for you," Liam said as he leaned in closely.

"I have everything I need." Emma smiled.

"Well that may be true, but I think you'll want this." He

reached into his pocket and pulled out a small box. "I found it at the castle. It belongs around your neck, right where I put it on our wedding day."

Liam opened the box and Emma saw her silver horseshoe necklace. Tears filled her eyes as he unfastened the clasp, which had been repaired, and placed the jewelry around her neck. She touched the smooth metal pendant with her fingertips, grateful it was resting once again where it belonged.

"I don't know about you, Em, but I'll take all the luck I can get. It might be a silly Irish superstition, but I'm not going to tempt fate." Liam grinned as he brushed Emma's lips with his.

"Neither am I. I love the necklace, but I know who my real lucky charm is, Liam. I'm married to him."

Emma closed her eyes and tasted the sweetness of her husband's lips. A few days ago, she'd been sure her good fortune had run out. She'd learned that a person could be tested beyond belief, but faith and love would always win out in the end. She understood that the ending of one thing was always the beginning of another, and if we try hard enough, we will always find the strength to carry on.

EPILOGUE

THERE WASN'T A SOUL AROUND THE DAY XAVIER'S NEARLY lifeless form washed onto the rocky shore of a remote beach on the Shetland Islands. His clothing was torn and tattered, and his skin had grown pale and ashen from the cold temperature of the water.

He coughed and sputtered as his damaged body came to rest on a large rock. The skin on his face was corroded, and the bones underneath were visible. He had a gaff hook sticking out of his eye socket. Anyone unfortunate enough to have seen the man would have been terrified. He barely appeared human. He was a monster, something from a nightmare.

The fact that he'd endured so long in the frigid water was nothing short of a miracle. A weaker man wouldn't have made it nearly that long. One might say it was sheer willpower that had allowed him to survive under those conditions. He tried to move his battered body, but it was no use. After days of barely hanging on, he knew his time had come to an end.

He glanced at his surroundings with his one good eye and

knew he'd made it. He'd said he was going to the Shetland Islands, and he had. But nothing had happened as it was supposed to. He should have been living out his dreams with the woman he loved, not dying alone on the shore.

He closed his eyes and pictured her beautiful face and lovely strawberry-blonde hair. The sound of the waves crashed all around him as he thought of the first time he'd seen her. She'd changed him that day. She'd given him a reason to live.

The whipping wind drowned out the faint sound of his voice as he breathed his last word.

"Emma."

THE END

THANKS

Thanks for reading *'Til Death Do Us Part* (The Vows Trilogy Book 3). I do hope you enjoyed Emma's story. I appreciate your help in spreading the word, including telling a friend. Before you go, it would mean so much to me if you would take a few minutes to write a review and share how you feel about my story so others may find my work. Reviews really do help readers find books. Please leave a review on your favorite book site.

Don't miss out on New Releases, Exclusive Giveaways and much more!

Join my newsletter: http://eepurl.com/cfhMXf
Like me on Facebook: www.facebook.com/heidireneemason
Join my reader group: Heidi's Tribe:
https://www.facebook.com/groups/346156819065335
Follow me on Twitter: @heidireneemason
Follow me on Instagram: @author_heidireneemason
Follow me on BookBub:
https://www.bookbub.com/authors/heidi-renee-mason

Visit my website for my current booklist:
www.heidireneemason.com

I'd love to hear from you directly, too. Please feel free to email me at: heidisbooks999@gmail.com or check out my website www.heidireneemason.com for updates.